SURVIVE THE NIGHT

SURVIVE THE NIGHT

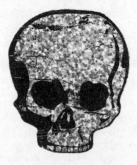

DANIELLE VEGA

razOr
bill

AN IMPRINT OF PENGUIN RANDOM HOUSE

razOr bill

An Imprint of Penguin Random House
Penguin.com

alloyentertainment

Produced by Alloy Entertainment
1325 Avenue of the Americas
New York, NY 10019

ISBN: 978-1-59514-725-7

Printed in the United States of America

1 3 5 7 9 10 8 6 4 2

Design by Liz Dresner

To the real Feelings Are Enough

ONE

DEAD PEOPLE DON'T REALLY LOOK LIKE THEY'RE sleeping.

I'm not an expert. I've only seen the one. She was my roommate at Mountainside Gardens Rehabilitation Center. Rachel, only she pronounced her name *Rock-el*. I used to say it wrong on purpose.

Rachel was a boozehound. I had to dump all my perfume because the nurses said she'd drink it once withdrawal set in. I thought they were full of it, but then Rachel found out this girl down the hall had nail polish remover. She snuck out one night and stole it.

I found her in our bathroom, slumped next to the toilet. Sweat drenched her bleached-blond hair, making it clump around her hollowed-out cheeks and blue-tinted face. Skinny red veins spiderwebbed over the whites of her eyes, and blood and snot dripped from her nose. Dried vomit clung to her chin and her cracked purple lips.

I didn't tell anyone outside of the clinic about Rachel. Not my parents. Not even Shana.

I also didn't tell anyone back home about Moira, who ate her own hair, or Cara, who screamed whenever you touched her, or Tori Anne, who begged for drugs even though all her teeth were rotting out of her skull. You can't tell people stories like that without giving them ideas.

Like, *That's really fucked up.*

Or, *What were you even doing there?*

Or, *Maybe you're just like them.*

"End of the road," I say. "Last house on the left."

Dad pulls our Subaru around the corner, past a wooden sign that reads FLYING EAGLE ESTATES. I press my face against the car window. Identical brick mini mansions spiral off in every direction, all surrounded by lush green grass and towering pine trees. When I was little, I used to think Madison's neighborhood looked like something out of a fairy tale. We'd spend hours darting across the pristine lawns and hiding behind gnarled old oak trees, pretending to be warrior princesses.

"I remember where Madison lives, Casey," Dad says. "You used to spend every weekend here."

I twirl the turtle charm on my necklace. I got it because of my last name, Myrtle, and also because I was going to study them back when I was planning on being a marine biologist. But marine biology means college, so who knows anymore. "You excited to see your friends?" Dad asks.

"Sure." I stretch the word into two syllables. How excited can you be to see "parent-approved" friends? I mean, really? Dad shoots me a look. "I *am*," I add, flashing my "normal teenage girl" smile. "Really."

Dad nods, but he doesn't look convinced. We have the same face: long, straight nose, stubby chin. We even have the same dark eyes and thick brows that tell the world exactly what we're thinking at every moment. Right now, his brows pinch in at the middle, creating tiny worry lines on his forehead.

I flip down the sun visor and scrutinize my reflection. Pale skin, circles under my eyes, and a fresh zit coming in on my forehead. I should have insisted on a post-rehab makeover.

I push my hair back to check out the freshly shaved side of my head. At least that still looks badass. I stole my dad's electric razor a couple of days after getting back and buzzed my brown locks. You can't see it when my hair is down, but Mom freaked anyway. Which was the entire point.

I make a face at my reflection and pinch my pale cheeks. A faint burst of red appears on my skin, then disappears a second later. I sigh and flip the sun visor up.

"Feeling okay?" Dad asks.

Translation: *Did the thousands of dollars we spent on Mountainside actually fix you?*

"I'm good. This is pie." Pie's my word. Kind of like "it's a piece of cake," only I used to scarf down these cherry–cream cheese pies my dad made every weekend.

It's also my classic nonanswer, and I feel guilty the second it's out of my mouth. "I feel stronger," I add.

"Well, I guess I'm glad," Dad says. I reach for the air conditioner and Dad drops his hand on mine before I can pull it away. He squeezes, his eyes still on the road. I let him leave his hand there for a full three seconds before shrugging it off.

We roll up to a white house with forest-green shutters and a wraparound front porch. Madison leans against one of the columns flanking the front door, her long, tan legs stretched out before her. All my old friends and soccer teammates crowd around her, talking and laughing.

It feels stuffy in the Subaru all of a sudden. I switch the air-conditioning off and roll my window down. Dad cuts the steering wheel to the left, pulling up alongside a row of freshly planted yellow tulips. I squirm, uncomfortably, in my seat.

"Something wrong?" Dad asks.

"No," I say, too fast. It's a scientific fact that dads don't understand teenage girl politics. Like how your former best friend might invite you to a sleepover just to be nice, and not because she actually wants to spend the night with the school cautionary tale.

I grab my polka-dot Herschel backpack and push the door open. The smell of tulips overwhelms me. It's like the way you imagine flowers smell, not how they *really* smell. Except these do.

Madison turns at the sound of the car door slamming. I step onto her lawn, and her face lights up.

"Casey!" she squeals. "You came!"

She hands her lemonade glass to the girl standing next to her and races across the sloped lawn toward me. Watching her, I feel a phantom twinge of pain in my knee, the injury that started this all. Madison throws her arms around my shoulders, and suddenly all I can see is tan skin and blond hair. She squeezes too tightly, giving me the feeling this hug is more for the girls on the porch and my dad than it is for me. I rock back on my heels.

"*Oof,*" I groan. She's not much larger than me, but she works out six times a week and never eats junk food. Her body is all muscle. *Life* is a contact sport for Madison.

Dad unrolls the car window. "Madison, it's nice to see you again," he says. Madison releases me from her strangle-hug. She's already wearing a pair of polka-dot pajama shorts and a loose-fitting T-shirt. He turns back to me and his eyebrows do the furrowing, worry-line thing again. "You have your cell, right? You'll call me if you need . . ."

"Anything," I finish for him. "I know. I will."

Dad stares at me for a beat too long, a nervous smile on his face. I should feel guilty about that smile. But I'm so tired of everyone looking at me like I'm a bomb about to go off.

I already *went* off. I'm better now.

Dad rolls his window up, waving one last time as he steers the car away from the curb. I wiggle my fingers at his taillights, halfheartedly.

"There's lemonade on the porch," Madison says, looping her arm around my shoulder. "And hummus and stuff."

She winds her thick blond braid around her finger. The gold "best friends" bracelet I gave her back in sixth grade dangles from her wrist. Something about it makes me sad. Like the strangle-hug made me sad. She's trying too hard to remind me that we're friends.

"Do you have Funfetti icing?" I ask, looking away from the bracelet. Funfetti was practically a fifth food group our freshman year.

"Ha," Madison says, and flicks the pendant on her bracelet. "Is it weird being back?"

"No, it's pie." I smooth my hair over the shaved side of my head. Shana said my old haircut didn't match my personality, but Madison wouldn't understand. She hasn't changed her hair since elementary school. "I'm doing good. Great, actually." I stop walking and lower my voice so the girls on the porch don't overhear me. "Look, I'm not really a drug addict. My parents overacted. They thought I was, like, shooting heroin into my eyeballs or something." I laugh, but it's stilted and awkward. Madison stares at me, frowning.

"Anyway," I continue, clearing my throat. "I just had a bad reaction to my painkillers." At least, I *think* I had a bad reaction to my painkillers. The night I went to rehab is a blank spot on my memory. I don't remember anything that happened, but Shana told me I passed out, and she said it could have been the pain meds, which is good enough for me. Apparently it happens all the time.

"I wasn't anything like the girls there," I finish, thinking of Rachel and Moira and Tori Anne.

Madison wrinkles her nose. She looks skeptical. "Painkillers can be addictive."

"Hence the rehab," I say. "And they were prescription, anyway." My doctor prescribed oxycodone after a girl the size of a Clydesdale slammed into me during a soccer game last year, ruining my knee. "My parents just flipped because I passed out, but my doctor said lots of people have bad reactions. It wasn't a big deal."

"I don't know. I'm not even eating white flour anymore," Madison says. "I read this article that says it's basically as addictive as cocaine."

I tug on my Myrtle necklace. What are you supposed to say to a girl who doesn't eat *bread*? That's not even human.

"Is there rehab for pasta?" I ask. Madison laughs too loudly for my stupid joke and takes the steps to the porch two at a time.

All the girls are already dressed in their pajamas, except for Stacy Donovan, who's wearing Nike athletic shorts and a neon blue sports bra. I'm pretty sure she was born wearing athletic shorts and a sports bra. She smiles at me when I step onto the porch.

"Cute jeans!" she calls.

"Um, thanks," I say. A pair of tight, dark-wash jeans with a ripped knee hangs low on my hips, accentuating my long legs and thin waist. I spent all afternoon trying on everything in my closet, and I finally landed on my best jeans and a slouchy black T-shirt.

"Do you want to get changed?" Madison asks. I glance down at my backpack. I brought my matching pj's with the giant strawberries on them, like I'm twelve.

"I'm good for now." I dump my backpack on the ground and take the glass of lemonade Madison offers me.

Kiki Charles waves from the porch swing, where she's sitting with Amanda Rice and a girl from the JV team I don't recognize. I wave back. Kiki and I used to partner up for early morning sprints, and Amanda always offered to paint my nails blue and yellow—the team colors—on the bus to away games. But that was all pre-injury, pre-Shana, pre-rehab. I barely saw them after I quit the team last year.

Amanda leans forward, balancing her lemonade glass on her knee. "Please tell me you're taking calc this year," she says. "Algebra 2 was horrible after you left. Mr. Nelson was up to two puns a day by the end of the year, and I had no one to groan with in the back row."

"Tragic," I say, and the corner of my mouth lifts into a smile. Talking about school is the high school girl equivalent of talking about the weather. But it's still better than the alternative.

"You have no idea," Amanda says. "Did you know he likes angles, but only to a certain *degree*? Ooh, and he kept threatening to kick Kevin Thomas out of class if he had another infraction." She shoots me a disgusted look over the top of her lemonade glass. "Get it? In*fraction*."

Madison rolls her eyes. "No one has suffered like you've suffered," she says.

I take a drink of lemonade, grimacing as I swallow. It's sugar-free. "So." I clear my throat, shrugging the tension from my shoulders. "What else have I missed?"

"Tuesday's now sloppy joe day in the cafeteria," Madison says with mock enthusiasm. "And Sean Davenport's dating Clare Ryan this week, so that's . . . special."

I frown, trying to picture our high school quarterback with Clare, the drama weirdo who wears a beret to school every day. "What happened to Sarah?"

"Sarah's a born-again Christian now," Kiki explains, wrinkling her nose. "That's a whole different drama. Oh, and Sam cut his hair. Have you seen—"

"I'm so behind already," I say, interrupting her before she can start talking about my ex-boyfriend. Madison slips an arm over my shoulder.

"I went to junior prom with Henry Frank and he spent the *entire* night making out with Lisa Jones in the third-floor stairwell," she says.

"Asshole." I tuck my hair behind my ear, flashing her a smile. I know she's trying to steer the conversation away from Sam, and I feel a rush of gratitude. It's almost like old times. Like in fifth grade when this girl in the cafeteria made fun of me for getting ketchup on my white tank top, and Madison retaliated by dumping a carton of chocolate milk over her head.

Then Amanda Rice leans forward, wrinkling her nose. "Did you shave your head?" she asks.

Shit. I push my fingers through my hair and touch the buzzed sides of my head. It feels like peach fuzz. "Not exactly."

"Did you do it in rehab?" Amanda asks. Madison shoots her a look—her "we talked about this" look. Which means they must've had an entire conversation about me before I even got here.

I look down at the ice melting in my lemonade glass, trying to ignore the heat climbing up the back of my neck.

I imagine Madison telling them not to ask me about rehab. Madison saying they should pretend everything's normal. That we're all still friends.

"It was just a question," Amanda mutters.

I smooth my hair over my ears. "I didn't do it in rehab."

"It looks, um, really different," Madison says in a fake cheery voice. "But whatever, right? It's just hair. It'll grow back."

"Yeah." I fumble with Myrtle and look down at my shoes. You should be allowed to scream in public whenever a conversation gets really awkward. And then time could reset itself and you get a do-over.

But I can't scream without everyone thinking I'm a crazy junkie, so I pinch the skin on my palm and stare at the mole in the middle of Amanda's forehead. She's still talking but her voice sounds like static. All I hear is a low buzz as she drones on.

The sound of a motor cuts through the hum. I turn to watch a rusty sky-blue Buick rumble up the street. I grin, recognizing Shana's car immediately. She inherited it when her grandmother got too old to drive. Her grandmother's CHASTITY IS FOR LOVERS sticker still decorates the back bumper, but Shana scratched out "lovers" with her keys and carved "fuckers" into the paint next to it. She left her grandmother's rosaries dangling from the rearview mirror but hot-glued the head of her little sister's My Little Pony to the car antenna.

Shana pulls up next to the curb, and the little horsey head wobbles above the car like crazy. Obnoxiously loud rock music drifts out of her cracked windows. Julie fills her cheeks with air and presses her lips against the back window. Aya sits next to her, eyes squeezed shut as she croons along with the music.

"Oy, Case!" Shana hollers. She honks, twice. "Get that cute little ass down here!"

The soccer girls go silent. Madison frowns.

"Are they drunk?" she asks.

"No," I say, although they probably are. Julie fogs up the back window with her breath and draws a penis in the steam. She doubles over with laughter. I start to smile, too, then bite my lip when I see the look on Madison's face.

"What are they *doing* here?"

"I don't know," I say. I really don't. I haven't seen Shana since getting back from rehab. She must've called my house to figure out where I was.

"Casey!" Shana lays on her horn. Without realizing I'm doing it, I pull my backpack up over my shoulder.

Madison freezes, a carrotful of hummus halfway to her mouth. "Wait, are you *leaving* with them?"

"I . . ." I hesitate.

The thing is, I never worry that Shana talks about me behind my back. If she had something to say, she'd say it to my face. And Shana would never invite me out just to be nice. Shana repels "nice" like water repels oil. She's the antithesis of nice. She's *real*.

I glance back at her car. She stares at me from the front seat, one eyebrow cocked. Like a dare.

"I'm sorry," I finish lamely.

"Whatever." Madison picks up her lemonade, shaking the ice at the bottom of the glass. The best friend charm glints on her wrist.

"The next time you have a sleepover . . ." I start, but Madison snorts and gives me a look that's pure venom.

"Sorry," I say again. I set my lemonade glass on the porch railing and start down the steps.

"Casey," Madison calls. I stop at the edge of her lawn and glance over my shoulder.

"Yeah?"

Madison stares at Shana's Buick. For a split second, I see things like she does: the rusted car that could break down at any moment, Shana drumming her hands against the steering wheel. Julie lighting a joint in the backseat.

Madison shifts her eyes back to me. I wind the backpack strap around my fingers, suddenly uncomfortable. I think of Rachel's puffy face and bloodshot eyes and have to clench my shoulders to keep from visibly cringing. I can't imagine what Madison sees when she looks at me. Only that I don't belong on her perfect lawn or in her perfect life. Not anymore.

Madison just shakes her head. "Be safe," she mutters.

TWO

I MET SHANA TWO DAYS AFTER SCREWING UP MY knee. I was slumped in a wheelchair in my hospital room. Alone. A thick cast covered my leg from ankle to mid-thigh, making it stick straight out in front of me.

The Voice blared from the TV mounted on my wall. Madison said she was going to call so we could watch it together, like we always did. But the show had started twenty minutes ago, and she had never called. Something squeaked outside my door. I glanced up and saw Shana watching from the hall.

Everyone at my school knew Shana. They said she had sex with our geometry teacher freshman year. She could get you weed and fake IDs. She skipped more classes than she attended. I'd heard her mom was a nurse at the hospital, but it was the first time I'd actually seen Shana here.

She sat outside my door in a wheelchair she obviously didn't need, her blue-tipped hair framing a pale, pointed face.

"Want one?" She held out a carton of cigarettes.

"We're in a hospital," I said.

"Oh. Right." She slid a thin black cigarette out of the pack and placed it between her lips. "Christ, what are you watching?"

"Something crappy." I only said it because I was pissed at Madison, and *The Voice* was her favorite show. But Shana smiled.

"Complete crap," she said. "This show is the crap that crap craps out."

I laughed. It was the first time I'd laughed all day. "I guess," I said. "It's not like I have anything better to do."

"Bullshit," she said, shaking her head. "Follow me."

She wheeled away without another word, chair squeaking. You know that story about the guy who plays his flute and all the kids follow him out of the city? That's how I felt. Like if I didn't follow Shana, everything would change. Or nothing would.

I wheeled after her, down the hall and out the back door, to a grassy stretch next to the dumpsters. I expected her to pull out a joint and offer me a hit.

Instead, she rolled to the edge of a hill. She glanced over her shoulder at me and wiggled her eyebrows.

"Look," she said. "No hands."

She launched herself down, lifting her arms high above her head. The wind distorted her scream, turning it feral. It blew her hair back in a rippling sheet of blue and blond. And then she was rattling down the hill. Her laughter bubbled above her, hanging in the air long after she disappeared.

I followed her to the edge, my heart pounding. I wanted everything she had—the hair, the laugh, the scream that sounded half wild. I launched myself over the side of the hill with a single push. A scream ripped from my throat and it sounded almost, but not quite, like hers.

My wheelchair rattled beneath me, threatening to fall apart. My stomach plunged and the wind made my eyes water. Adrenaline charged through my body, but then it was over, and I was rolling to a stop next to Shana. A wide smile cut across my face.

More, I thought.

Shana looked back at me, eyes glinting. "Tell me you didn't love that," she said.

I hurry away from Madison's house, trying to ignore the whispers that erupt behind me as soon as I'm out of earshot. This will be all over school on Monday. Not that it matters. Rehab did a pretty good job of destroying my reputation already.

I pull open the door to Shana's rusty Buick.

"Hey, slut," Shana says, winking at me. Platinum blond

hair frames her face, but now the tips are dyed bright pink instead of blue. Thick eyeliner circles her eyes. I can't help smiling as I slide into her car. It doesn't really matter what Madison and the rest of my old soccer friends think about me. Shana makes them look like little kids.

"Bitch," I say, and Shana's lips curl into an amused smirk. They're slathered with pink lipstick the same shade as her hair.

"Rehab made you feisty," she says, wrinkling her nose at me.

I brush an empty Funyuns bag off the passenger seat and pull the door shut. Madison and the rest of my old friends watch from her porch. I turn away from them, heat climbing up my neck.

"Let's go," I say. "They're staring."

"Because they're *jealous*." Shana's voice is always a shock the first few times you hear it. It's deep and gravelly—the voice of a forty-year-old smoker, not a high school girl. She's talked her way into bars and clubs all across Philly. Which is insane, since she's a tiny pixie of a human being. Underneath all the makeup, she looks like she's thirteen years old.

"Don't you realize how hot we are?" Shana says. I roll my eyes, but her words loosen something in my chest. It's the way she says *we*. The way she thinks I'm more like her than I am like Madison.

She pulls away from the curb, blowing Madison a kiss

as we roll past her house. She says, "I don't think it's an exaggeration to say we could get the entire state of Pennsylvania to bow down and worship us."

I twist around to face the back. "Hey, guys!"

"Stop. Too much energy." Julie yawns. She's stretched across the backseat, a bare foot propped against Aya's leg. Her bushy mane of hair falls past her hips. Only one eye peeks out beneath the crazy curls.

"Sorry!" I grin, tapping my fists against the back of my seat. All the nerves and anxiety I felt walking up the stairs to Madison's porch have disappeared. I feel relaxed for the first time since leaving Mountainside. No one is judging me here.

"So," I say. "Where are we going?"

"Jesus, do you want an itinerary?" Shana rearranges her loose, gauzy tunic so the neckline falls over her shoulder. I can see her black bra through the fabric. "Does it matter?"

"No. It's pie." I shift in my seat. If my parents find out I ditched Madison's sleepover, I'll be grounded for the rest of my life, but I push that out of my mind.

"We rescued you from suburban hell," Aya adds. She squints at Julie's foot, a nail polish wand clutched in her manicured fingers. Three toenails are already fluorescent pink. "Aren't you excited to see us?"

Instead of answering, I crawl halfway into the backseat and plant a messy kiss on Aya's cheek. "Mwuah!"

"Hey!" Aya giggles, and shoves the wand back into the polish, screwing the cap shut. "Watch the—Oh my God, what did you do to your hair?"

I touch the side of my head, and nerves start flickering through my stomach again. Shana jerks around to look at me, and the entire car swerves. I start to push my hair down over the buzzed side, but she grabs my arm.

"Don't be shy." Her fingernails cut into my wrist. "Let's see."

"It's not a big deal," I say. But I brush my hair back behind my ear. Wind leaks in from the cracked window and tickles my skull. Shana cackles and drops my hand.

"You look completely deranged," she says. She pulls out of Madison's neighborhood and hits the gas. I jerk forward, catching myself a second before I slam into the dashboard.

"Is that a good thing?" My voice sounds needy, which I hate. Shana has this way of looking at you when you do something lame. Like she's trying to solve a math problem. Like you don't quite add up. I glance at her, preparing myself for The Look. But she grins.

"Are you kidding? It's *amazing*." She squints at me. "Why? Didn't those boring little soccer girls like it?"

"I think they were confused by it."

Shana throws her head back and laughs.

"Of course they were," she says. She wraps a pink strand of hair around her finger. "Fuck 'em. You look like one of us now."

I grin and push my hair to one side to better show off my buzz. Shana nods her approval.

"Completely deranged," she says again. This time it sounds like a good thing. Like something to aspire to.

"If I rub it, can I make a wish?" Julie asks. Aya snorts.

"That's not the first time she's said that today," Aya adds. Julie smacks her on the shoulder.

"Why are you painting her toes in the car?" I ask, shifting my attention back to them.

"I thought we might need road-trip activities." Aya purses her perfectly lined cherry-red lips. I stare at her mouth, jealous. I can't wear lipstick without smearing it everywhere. I blame my parents. I wasn't allowed to wear makeup until I was sixteen.

Aya wrinkles her nose at Julie's foot. "On second thought, the pink makes your skin look green."

"I think it's rad," Julie says, wiggling her toes.

Shana's car skids to a stop at a red light, and my head slams against my headrest.

"Oops. Sorry," Shana says with mock sincerity. When I first started hanging with Shana, I used to bitch whenever she went over the speed limit or rolled through stop signs. But that just made her drive like more of a maniac.

21

Shana grabs my backpack and pulls it onto her lap. "What did you pack for the sleepover?"

I cringe, thinking of my strawberry pj's. "Nothing," I say, reaching for my bag. The light turns green and Shana's car jerks forward.

"No, let me see." She steers with one hand and yanks my backpack open with the other. She pulls out my pajamas and smirks. "These are *precious*."

I want to die. I snatch my backpack from Shana's lap, but she holds the pajamas out of my reach. She grins, wickedly, and unrolls her window.

My stomach drops. "What are you doing?" I hiss.

"Liberating you," she says. She thrusts my pj's out the window, her fingers clenched tightly around the cotton shorts and tank top. They flap in the wind like strawberry-print flags.

"Shana, don't," I say.

"Casey! Maybe Madison and those other girls *love* their adorable matching sleepwear, but you're nothing like them." Shana shakes her head, like she sees something in me that I don't. "You are oversize band T-shirts. You're black thongs and men's boxers."

Her words stir something inside me. It's like she's describing a completely different world from the one I grew up in. Her world is exotic and daring and sexy. It's seductive.

Shana glances at me, her eyebrow cocked. "Do you

really want them back?" she asks. I roll my lower lip between my teeth. I glance at the pink pajamas, then back at Shana.

"Do it," I say. Shana grins and lets go.

The pink cotton shorts and tank top whip away from the Buick, narrowly missing the windshield of a white minivan before fluttering to the pavement. I watch them grow smaller, and it's like a weight has been lifted.

"You're psychotic," I mutter. But I'm smiling.

"Face it, you're going to lead an incredibly exciting and dangerous life." She winks at me. "Whether you want to or not."

Exciting. It makes me think of discovering secret clubs in the city and partying with dangerous people and dating older men.

But then Rachel's bloated, vacant face pops into my mind. I squeeze my eyes shut, trying to force the image away. There has to be a way to live an exciting life without winding up like her.

I look around for a distraction and my eyes fall on the book wedged beneath Julie's thigh. I grab it from her and flip through the pages.

"This is in French," I say. Julie nods.

"Yeah," she says in her slow, even drawl. "It is."

"But you don't speak French," I point out.

Julie purses her lips, tapping a finger against her chin. The black onyx ring she always wears glitters at me. "The meaning of the book transcends language," she says.

"I don't get it either," Aya says. She pulls a tiny silver compact from her purse and checks to make sure her chignon is still perfect. She adjusts the silky scarf tied around her head so the bow is right below her left ear. "She's been weird ever since her brother brought her this weed from Colorado."

"Hey," Julie says, frowning. "I was weird *long* before that."

Aya rolls her eyes. Neon blue liner wings away from the corners of her lids, the lines so perfect they look like art. Aya has a beauty channel on YouTube. She only has ten thousand followers now, but we all know she'd be famous if she put a little effort into it.

"Why are we talking about you two? You're boring." Shana swerves in front of a white SUV. A horn blares. "I want to hear *all* about rehab," she says, flipping off the SUV over her shoulder. "Did you screw any of the nurses?"

"The nurses were all female," I say. Shana blinks.

"So did you screw any of the nurses?" she asks again. Julie groans and flops back against the window.

"I heard lots of girls experiment in rehab," Shana says.

"You're thinking of college," Aya interrupts, examining her cuticles. "You can't start sleeping with girls until you spend thousands of dollars getting an art history degree. Everyone knows that."

"What if I don't go to college?"

"Then you'll just have to stick with boys," I say, grateful for the subject change. Shana pretends to pout. She shifts gears and merges onto Oldtown Highway. I watch the speedometer needle shoot from fifty-five to seventy.

"So. What's new?" I ask before Shana can start asking about rehab again. "I hear Sarah Johnson's a Christian now?"

Julie snickers. "That girl is *dumb*. I told her I was an atheist, and she said she didn't know there was an atheist church in town."

"Hand me my bag," Shana says, waving at the slouchy leather hobo bag on the floor next to my feet. I thrust it toward her and she pulls out a tiny bottle of Jack Daniel's. She takes a swig, then hands it to me.

"I'm okay, actually," I say, waving the bottle away. The needle on the speedometer's hovering around eighty now, but I resist the urge to buckle my seat belt, knowing that Shana would notice.

Shana groans. "*Please* tell me you're not going to be all boring now?"

"She just got back," Aya says. "Give her a break."

"What?" Shana rolls her eyes. "She went for *drugs*, not alcohol."

I feel a twinge of irritation. It's like she thinks I got back from summer camp, not *rehab*. "You know, I saw some really messed up shit in there."

"You think *I* haven't seen messed up shit?" Shana catches Aya's eye in the rearview mirror and tosses the whiskey bottle over her shoulder.

"Watch the road," I mutter. We're at eighty-five now.

"I guess it's kind of adorable," Shana continues, smirking. "Little suburban princess got all freaked by the scary addicts." She glances at me, and her voice hardens. "Do you, like, not want to hang with us anymore?" Her jaw tightens. "You didn't even call when you got home."

She actually looks hurt. Guilt oozes into my chest.

"You know how my parents are," I say. Shana doesn't look at me, and my stomach clenches. "Of course I still want to be your friend. Jesus."

Shana cocks an eyebrow. "Prove it."

Aya nudges me with the whiskey bottle. I slide it from her fingers and take a small sip. Even so, it strings my throat and makes my eyes water. Shana rolls her eyes.

"Or you could take a big girl drink," she challenges.

"I haven't had a drink in, like, twelve weeks." Still, I take a larger swig.

"Good girl," Shana purrs.

"Casey's trying to find some balance." Julie pinches her fingers together like she's mediating. "We should support her."

Aya snort-laughs into her hand. "What are you—like, a guru?" she asks. Julie cracks a smile.

"Call me Mother Julie. I'll teach you the secrets of life."

"Casey doesn't need balance," Shana cuts in. "She needs her parents to loosen the fuck up." She looks at me for confirmation. "You know you didn't need rehab. Your parents flipped for absolutely no reason."

"I know," I mutter. My parents are the only people on the planet who think oxycodone is some big scary drug. It was bullshit when they sent me away to rehab like a common junkie and not just a regular teenage girl having a little fun.

Then again, nail polish remover isn't a big scary drug, either, and look what it did to Rachel.

I try to come up with something else to say. Something that'll convince Shana we can still rule all of Pennsylvania, even if I'm sober. "It was just creepy as hell in there," I finally say. "I don't want to end up like those girls."

Oldtown Highway narrows to two lanes. We call this stretch the Noose because the road curves in a big loop before merging with I-276, the interstate that'll take us the rest of the way to New York City. The highway here is narrow enough that you have to con-centrate to stay in your lane. At least once a year some kid takes the Noose too fast and drives into oncoming traffic.

Shana slows as we curve around and roll up behind a rusted Jeep Cherokee going twenty miles below the speed limit. She swears under her breath and hits the turn signal, swerving into the oncoming lane to pass.

"Careful," I mutter.

"What do you mean *careful*?" Shana glances sideways at me. "Afraid I'm going to crash?"

We shoot past the Cherokee, but she doesn't pull back into her lane. Anxiety prickles up my spine. "A little," I admit.

Shana gets a strange glint in her eye. "Maybe I *should*," she says. "Maybe I should crash this car and let it burn." She presses down on the gas.

"Ha, ha." I say. Shana presses down harder.

"You think I'm joking?" she asks. The speedometer needle crawls past eighty-five. The Buick starts to tremble.

"Dude, I don't think your car's supposed to go this fast," Julie says. "It's going to fall apart."

"You're fine, aren't you, boy?" Shana purrs, petting the dashboard. She presses harder, and the needle climbs to ninety. My fingers itch to reach for my seat belt, but I just curl them around my seat.

"Maybe if we hit one hundred, we'll fly." She smiles this little-kid smile that takes up half her face. I don't know anyone else who smiles like Shana does: it's pure, giddy joy. Like she doesn't care who sees her. The speedometer needle ticks up to ninety-five.

Headlights appear in the distance. They flicker through the trees, white and haunting.

"Shana . . ." Aya says from the backseat.

"I see them," she says. A red pickup appears at the far end of the curved road, driving toward us.

"Maybe we should stop," I say. Shana winks at me.

"We're playing chicken," she says.

I dig my fingers into the car seat, trying not to notice how quickly the trees race past my window. I'm starting to feel sick.

"Get back in your lane," I say. I think of the videos they made us watch in Driver's Ed. One of them was about how seat belts could be the only thing to keep you alive in a head-on collision. I pull my seat belt over my lap and click it into place, no longer worried about seeming cool. Shana snickers.

Aya leans forward and wraps her fingers around my headrest. "This isn't funny," she says.

Shana throws her head back and hoots with laughter.

Julie giggles and starts humming the *Jaws* theme song. The rearview mirror rattles like it might fall off, and I notice a crack jutting across Shana's windshield. If we crash into that pickup, the Buick will crumple around us like paper. I glance at the dashboard, wondering if this piece of crap car even has air bags.

The truck races closer. It flashes its brights at us, but Shana makes no move to swerve back into her lane. Pressure builds in my ears. They feel like they're about to pop.

"Shana!" I say again. We can't be more than a mile from the truck. I breathe in through my nose and out through my mouth, like they taught us in rehab. Half a mile.

A scream rises in my throat. The truck flashes its brights again. Shana leans into her horn. I squeeze my eyes shut, and the long, low sound echoes in my head.

I brace myself for the impact. The Buick jerks to the right. It rocks beneath me and bounces over something, then slows to a stop. Adrenaline races through my veins, and my heart beats jackrabbit fast. I ease my eyes open.

We're pulled over on the side of the road. The pickup speeds away, quickly becoming a tiny red dot. Pine trees tower over us.

Shana stares at me, her face bright and excited. "*Tell* me you didn't love that," she says. Aya swears, and Julie laughs so hard she starts to hiccup.

"Bitch," I say, collapsing against my seat. Fear pricks my skin like needles and my breath comes in ragged, sharp-edged bursts. I thought we were going to die.

But we didn't.

My blood burns hot as I turn those words over in my head. I didn't die. In fact, I feel more alive than I have in three months.

Shana smiles at me again, the same giddy, little-kid smile as before.

"I hate you," I say, smacking her on the shoulder. I try to glare, but I can't help it. Shana's smile is addictive.

Everything about her is addictive. The corner of my mouth twitches.

"I told you," she says. "You're going to lead an exciting, dangerous life. Just stick with me."

THREE

JULIE WIGGLES THE CAR DOOR HANDLE. "SHANA, does this thing even lock?"

We're parked on a narrow street behind a Food & Fun supermarket. A brick apartment building towers over us. Someone on the third floor has hung a Tommy Hilfiger beach towel in front of his window instead of curtains.

"Don't bother." Shana leans against the Buick, lighting a cigarette. "It doesn't start unless you know how to turn the screwdriver in the ignition *just* right. And I'm taking that secret to the grave."

I shake my head and stare down at the map on my phone. Shana still hasn't told me where we're going, but according to my phone we're somewhere in Brooklyn, just a few blocks from the Cog Factory, this under-18 club she loves. I don't get the secrecy. I've been to the Cog with her at least a dozen times.

Shana winks at me and blows cigarette smoke at my face. I hold my breath to keep from coughing. She smokes black clove cigarettes that smell like pine needles and vanilla.

"Miss it?" she asks. I quit during rehab, but I never *really* liked cigarettes. I always imagined smoke clinging to my lungs and turning them black. Shana loves smoking. She says it feels like breathing fire.

I heave an exaggerated sigh and wave the smoke away. "Don't tempt me," I say.

Shana laughs and takes another puff. Her skintight leather pants cling to her hips, and her black bra is perfectly visible beneath her gauzy white tunic.

I glance down at my own outfit. Aya thought my look was too boring to go with my new hair, so she let me borrow these long, silvery necklaces. I layered dozens of them over my loose T-shirt, grateful that I at least wore cute jeans tonight. Aya smudged dark makeup around my eyes and ran this goopy cream through my hair, making it fall to the side of my head in tousled waves. She said it makes my buzzed hair look fierce.

Shana takes the cigarette out of her mouth, and her lipstick leaves bright pink kiss marks behind. She cocks an eyebrow, considering me.

"What's up with the turtle?" she asks, touching the

Myrtle pendant still dangling from my neck. I wrap my hand around it.

"It's like a good luck charm," I say. I have a sudden vision of Shana ripping the pendant from my neck and tossing it down the gutter, so I tuck it beneath my T-shirt. "Better?"

Shana shrugs. "It makes your shirt bunch," she says, pushing herself off the side of the car. "This way."

We walk past a park and turn down a narrow alley lined with squat brick buildings that look abandoned. A cat weaves around dumpsters and mews at us before scurrying beneath a chain-link fence. The wind blows a grocery bag across the street.

"Brooklyn's kind of gross." Aya sidesteps an abandoned Styrofoam container filled with leftover Chinese food.

"Hey, that's *culture*," Julie says.

I see the Cog Factory sitting at the end of the street, and any doubt I had about where we're headed vanishes. A dirt-encrusted garage door makes up the front wall. During the day the place looks abandoned, but the door's open now, revealing a club the size of a walk-in closet. Layers of band posters, neon flyers, and stickers paper the walls, along with a few dozen rusted gears that could probably give you tetanus if you were dumb enough to touch them.

I feel music vibrating through the street as we walk closer, but it takes a second before I recognize the song. I freeze in the middle of the sidewalk, dread oozing through my body.

"That's *Sam's* band," I say. Shana whirls around.

"Surprise!" she says, throwing her hands over her head.

"No." I shake my head. This isn't happening. The last time I saw Sam was the day he dumped me. He had an eyelash stuck to his cheek, and all I could think about was how I wasn't allowed to brush the eyelash away.

There are lots of things you can't do when you aren't someone's girlfriend anymore. Brush away an eyelash, for instance. And you absolutely, one-hundred-percent *cannot* show up at his band's show unannounced. Crazy, desperate ex-girlfriends do that. Not me.

"Shana, we have to go," I say. I take a step backward. "*Now.* Before anyone can tell him we were here."

A smile cuts across her face. "Don't be silly."

"You don't understand." I clutch my stomach, suddenly feeling like I've been punched in the gut. I never should have left Madison's. I'm being punished for being a crappy friend and disobeying my parents. "We've only been broken up for, like, three months. This *cannot* happen."

I yank my necklace out from under my T-shirt and rub my thumb over Myrtle's sterling silver shell. Shana stares at the turtle. She makes her math-problem face. Shit.

"Sweetie." She speaks slowly, like she's talking to a toddler. She takes my hand and squeezes. "It's okay. You were invited."

"Invited?" I shake my head, certain I heard her wrong. "By who?"

"Who do you think?" Shana says. "I told Sam you were coming home this weekend, and he mentioned that you should drop by tonight."

"He said that?" The nerves in my stomach unclench. I study Shana's face. "Really?"

"*Really* really." She holds her hand over her heart, Pledge of Allegiance style. I swallow. My throat feels strangely dry.

"If this is some kind of trick . . ." I say.

"You're so paranoid." Shana rolls her eyes. "Now come on. If you don't show he's going to think you're blowing him off."

I move forward, hesitant. Shana treats the truth like it's Play-Doh, stretching it into new and ridiculous shapes until you have no idea what she started with. But what could she gain by lying about this? She doesn't even like Sam's band. Maybe he really did invite me. Maybe he wants to see me.

"Wait, I need your arm," Aya mumbles, grabbing my elbow. She's balanced on spiky, electric blue heels. Julie stares at them as she teeters past.

"How do you stand in those?" she asks.

"Practice," Aya says. Her blue leopard-print dress rustles next to my leg. Tulle makes the skirt stand straight out, like a prom dress from the fifties. Aya describes the look as eighties diva meets extra from the set of *Grease*.

I stare, wishing I'd at least worn a skirt. Or is it better that I didn't dress up? I tug at my T-shirt, ignoring the nerves prickling through my fingers. I look casual this way. Like it's just another Friday night.

I'm still dissecting my outfit when we stop outside the club. Teenagers crowd inside and spill onto the sidewalk. I huddle behind them and rise to my tiptoes, squinting into the dark for Sam.

Shana stops next to me. "You aren't really planning on standing out here," she says. "Like a commoner?"

"The place is packed," I say. Shana rolls her eyes.

"Did rehab scramble your brain? I've got moves."

I wrinkle my nose. "Did you really just say *moves*?"

Shana slips her hand into mine and squeezes. "Ready?"

Anxiety flutters through my chest. "Ready for what?"

"Take a deep breath." Shana drops her cigarette and stubs it out with the toe of her slouchy, eighties-style boot. Then, taking a comically large breath, she tunnels through the crowd, tugging me along behind her.

Julie calls for us to wait up, but Shana doesn't slow down. Elbows and hips jab into us, and a few people swear as we push farther into the club.

"Excuse us," Shana says. We shoulder past a group of boys in baseball caps. "She has epilepsy!" she shouts, giggling.

"I don't!" I call back, but we're already too far away

for them to hear me. Shana squeezes my hand until the bones in my fingers pinch together. She doesn't stop moving until we've positioned ourselves directly in front of the stage.

"There," she says. A tall girl wearing harem pants mutters "*bitch*" under her breath and sneers at us.

I barely even hear her. Sam—*my* Sam—stands a yard away, his shoulders arched over his bass guitar. Waves of nerves crash over me. A sweaty strand of hair falls over his face and *oh my God* I forgot how freaking gorgeous he is. He's rolled his sleeves up, so I can see his muscles tense as he plays, and his T-shirt sticks to the small of his back, revealing a narrow line of skin above the waistband of his jeans. My cheeks burn.

His fingers fly over the strings, his eyes narrowed in concentration. I've never loved anything the way Sam loves music. It used to make me jealous actually. I'd try out all these weird hobbies, like ceramics or poetry or drama. I figured I'd eventually find something that consumed me the way guitar consumed Sam. It took me a long time to realize that kind of passion doesn't happen for everyone. Sam had a gift. A tiny worry line appears on his forehead. My fingers itch to reach forward and smooth it out.

"I'm bar bound," Shana whisper-shouts into my ear. I motion for her to get me a can of soda, and she nods and tunnels through the crowd again.

Sam dances across the stage, head bobbing along with

the heavy indie rock his band, Feelings Are Enough, is known for. He rocks his shoulder forward and taps his foot, and I suddenly realize I've been staring for three minutes straight. And I'm just *standing* here. Everyone else is dancing, but I'm rooted to the spot. Like a zombie.

I force myself to move in time with the beat, pumping my arms over my head and hopping in place. Sweaty people crowd around me, crooning along with lyrics I know by heart. The music melts my nerves. I sing with them, shaking my shoulders and wiggling my hips.

I used to come to Sam's shows every weekend and stand in the front row, listening to the other girls whisper about how *hot* the bassist was. *That's my boyfriend*, I'd think. People say that teenagers never realize how lucky they are. But with Sam, I knew. Meeting him was like winning the lottery. My chest pinches. I close my eyes.

I first saw Sam lying in the grass outside a house party, his feet propped against a riding lawn mower. Long brown hair curled around his ears and hung over his tanned forehead. I'd never made the first move with a guy before, but with Sam I couldn't help it. My feet started toward him on their own, leaving me no choice in the matter.

"Do you work here?" I asked. Sam pushed himself onto one elbow and considered me through squinted eyes. He seemed to be studying my face, almost like he expected there to be a quiz later.

"I'm the safe-ride-home guy," he said.

"I thought only youth groups and sororities did that."
I kicked the mower's tires. "You're giving people rides
home on *this*?"

Sam leapt to his feet like he was spring-loaded. "*This
is a 1972 John Deere 112 with a Kohler engine and an
electric deck lift*," he said, touching the mower lovingly. "I
call her Matilda."

I watched his fingers caress the steering wheel. Heat
crept into my cheeks. "Of course," I said, clearing my
throat. "I drive a golf cart named Kevin."

Sam cocked an eyebrow. "Seriously?"

"No."

Sam laughed. "Yeah, well, I can't afford a real car yet."
He scratched the back of his head. His eyes crinkled at the
corners when he smiled. "Besides, I think I can convince
drunk people it's a roller-coaster ride."

He had me convinced. I ran my hand over the mower's
leather seat, imagining a late-night ride around the neighborhood, my arms wrapped around Sam's waist. Maybe
an unscheduled stop near a secluded grove of trees.

"Does Matilda handle well?" I asked.

Sam leaned in closer. His arm brushed against my shoulder. "Like a dream," he said. My throat suddenly felt thick.

"Lucky mower."

A chord cuts through the heavy rock, pulling me back
to the present. My eyes fly open and I realize that Sam's
only a few feet away. Watching me.

Every nerve in my body buzzes. His gaze feels like a physical thing. I shift in place, suddenly uncomfortable. He keeps his eyes trained on me for a fraction of a second longer, then turns away without so much as a nod or a smile.

Shana reappears, holding two cans of Coke.

"Refreshments," she says, passing me a soda. I tear my eyes away from Sam and take the can from her, my cheeks burning. I want the floor to open up and swallow me whole. The corner of my eye twitches. I blink, telling myself I will not—*cannot*—cry.

Shana produces the bottle of Jack and tips some into my drink. I don't even bother protesting.

"Just a little," I mutter. Shana lifts an eyebrow.

"You okay?" she asks. I glance at Sam, then back to Shana.

"He won't even look at me," I say. "I thought you said he wanted me to come tonight."

Shana takes a swig of Jack. She swallows, making a face.

"He did," she says, shoving the bottle back into her bag. "He told me to bring you. Just give him some time."

"I've been in rehab for two and a half months," I say. I can't help the bitterness that creeps into my voice. "How much time does he need?"

"A couple hours?" Shana leans toward me and tucks a strand of hair behind my ear. "He's seeing you again for the first time in months. He probably feels just as weird about it as you do."

Hope flickers through my chest. "You think?"

"Casey Myrtle, you are hot and amazing and every guy in this room is probably already in love with you." Shana hiccups and raises a hand to her mouth, giggling. "If stupid Sam can't see that, you're too good for him."

I roll my lower lip between my teeth. *Or he's too good for me*, I think. Before I can say another word, Aya and Julie push through the crowd to join us.

"*And* she didn't even get us a soda," Julie says, scowling at Shana. She already looks disheveled. Sweat smudges the eyeliner Aya drew on her in the car, and her curls stick out in funny angles. Something drips from her black tank top.

"Did you swim here?" Shana asks, giggling. Julie groans and tries to flatten her hair.

"Some jerk spilled his drink on me," she says.

"I offered her my Tide pen," Aya says, smoothing her hair back behind her ears. I notice that she, somehow, still looks perfect.

"My shirt is *wet*, not stained." Julie pinches the fabric away from her chest. "Disgusting," she mutters.

"Here. Take this," I say, handing my Coke to Julie. "I'll get two more."

I turn around and wind through the crowd. I need a moment alone, anyway. I know Shana was trying to be nice, but she couldn't possibly understand how I feel.

She goes through guys like they're nothing. But Sam isn't nothing. Sam is special.

Someone grabs my shoulders and whips me around.

A huge man looms over me. His fingers dig into my arms, pinning me in place. Thick white makeup covers his face. He's drawn black diamonds over his eyes and lined his lips in bloodred lipstick.

"Excuse me!" I try to pull away, but the man's hands are like vise around my arms. He doesn't wear a shirt, just rainbow suspenders strapped over his bare, hairy chest.

"*Shh!*" he says, pressing a meaty finger to my lips. His skin smells like sweat and earth. I cringe, and vomit rises in my throat. I try not to stare at his chipped yellow fingernail.

"Please," I say. He yanks me away from the bar with massive, muscular arms, muttering something under his breath. I try, again, to fight him off, but his body is solid and hard. It's like punching the wall.

"What are you doing?" I ask. I want to scream but the music's too loud. No one would hear me. The man's eyes dart across my face, hungrily. Makeup runs down his cheeks in streams, and bushy red hair surrounds his face. I beat at his shoulder with my fist. "Let me go!"

"Where are you going to go, little girl?" he asks, grinning to display a row of rotten teeth. He leans close to my face, and his smell makes my eyes water. It's sweat and beer and flesh baking in the sun.

"Please," I say again, my voice cracking. The man cackles. He thrusts his long, purple-stained tongue out from between his lips and runs it up my cheek.

"Don't you want to play?" he whispers into my ear.

FOUR

SPIT DRIES ALONG MY CHEEK. I'M DESPERATE TO
wipe it away, but the man's sticky fingers dig into my
arms, pinning me in place. A tattoo of a snake eating a rat
twists around his wrist.

I want to scream, but music throbs around me, drown-
ing my voice. I scan the crowd. Someone has to see what's
happening. Someone *has* to help. A girl with long blond
hair gyrates in front of me, and a guy with thick mutton-
chops stands next to the bar. Neither of them looks my
way. Another cry rises in my throat.

"Quiet, pretty." The man's rot-and-beer-scented breath
wafts over me. He clamps a hand over my lips, and fear
rockets through my body. I picture my parents sobbing
in the police station, my face on Missing Person posters. I
didn't think this sort of thing happened in real life. But the

man is very real. Lipstick seeps into every crack around his too-dry mouth, making it look like he's bleeding. I squirm, but he pulls me closer, until I'm pressed against his hairy chest. I stare at him in horror.

He moves his hand to the side of my face and cocks his eyebrow. Then he pulls a sparkler out of my ear—like magic. He drops my arm and produces a cheap gas station lighter with the other hand. I try to slip away, but the man angles his body in front of me. The sparkler crackles to life, shooting blue flames. My heart leaps in my chest.

The club around us falls eerily quiet as everyone turns to watch the crackling sparkler. The song ends and even the band seems to take notice.

The man claps his hands together, sending a spray of blue sparks to the floor. I jump back, knocking my hip against the bar. His red-painted lips part in a manic grin.

"You're *all* invited to play!" He spreads his arms wide and spins on the ball of one foot. "The second Survive the Night rave happens tonight," the man says. "Midnight."

Someone catcalls. The man waves the sparkler over his head and dances through the club. He steps out the door and onto the street, his blackened toes curling on the dirty sidewalk. The glittering blue sparkler disappears into the night.

My horror fades. It was a publicity stunt. *Jesus*.

The music starts up, and I push my way back through concertgoers who've started dancing again now that the clown man is gone. A pins-and-needles feeling pricks my arms and legs. A guy wearing a white fedora touches my shoulder.

"Hey, you okay?" he asks. I flash him a wobbly smile.

"Peachy," I say. I shove up to the bar. "Can I get a glass of water, please?" I ask the tattooed, lip-ringed bartender. She nods and disappears.

The guy in front of me hops off his stool, and I slide past him to steal it before anyone else can. I pull my purse onto my lap, my fingers trembling as I try to work the zipper. I swear under my breath and clench and unclench my hands until the trembling fades. I dig out my bottle of Tylenol and pop it open, shaking two small white tablets onto my palm. The bartender sets a water glass in front of me. I thank her and toss the pills back, taking a deep drink.

A girl with spiky green hair perches on the stool next to mine, her back to me while she talks with a curvy girl whose shaved head gleams in the dim light.

". . . so many rumors about Survive the Night," she's saying. I cock my head toward her, listening. "I can't believe anyone would actually go."

The girl with the shaved head removes a flask from inside her leather jacket and tosses back a swig. Technically the Cog is dry, but everyone sneaks in booze. I take another drink of water.

"Are you kidding?" The girl tucks the flask back into

her pocket. "Jenny said *everyone* was at the last one. She talked about it for a month."

Shana bursts out of the crowd and grabs my shoulders. She's wearing an orange baseball hat I've never seen before; the color clashes with her pink hair. Her heavily lined eyes look positively gleeful.

I flick the hat with my finger. "What the hell?"

"What? I made friends." Her gaze shifts to the Tylenol bottle sitting on the bar next to me. She cocks an eyebrow.

"I had a headache," I mutter. I take another drink of water and set the half-empty glass down on the bar.

"Jumpy, much?" she asks.

I think she's talking about the Tylenol again, but she nods at my foot. I'm tapping it against the bar so hard that my glass shudders, the water rippling. I hadn't even noticed. I drop a hand on my knee.

"Maybe a little." That's an understatement. I've been buzzing since that man grabbed me. I keep waiting for the adrenaline to fade but, if anything, it feels stronger. Energy courses through my arms and legs. It's like I need to *do* something to get rid of it. I slide to the edge of my bar stool. "Let's dance."

Shana takes my wrists and pulls me to my feet. She spins me in a circle. I giggle, trying not to crash into the person behind me.

"We should go," she says, her eyes glinting with

excitement. My smile freezes. I don't have to ask what she's talking about. Before rehab, I'd been dying to go to some illegal underground rave. But raves mean drugs.

"Remember what I said about taking it easy tonight?" I remind her.

She frowns and leans forward. "Don't I always take care of you?" She rubs my buzzed head, grinning. "Remember the pool party?"

"Of course I remember."

A few of months ago, Shana had dragged us all to this rave at an empty pool. Three concrete diving towers soared above the party. A bunch of kids crowded on top of them, dancing as close to the edges as they dared.

The highest platform rose nearly forty feet in the air. No one was brave enough to go up there, but I was drunk and a little high and I wanted to do something dangerous. I wanted to feel alive.

I still remember how the wind whipped my hair around my ears and the way my heart thudded in my chest as I climbed. I felt invincible. Like I could fly.

Then, halfway up the ladder, I looked down.

The people below were tiny, like plastic army men. My eyes clouded, and all at once, I realized how high I was, how sweaty my palms were. The wind was too strong, and the ladder felt rickety beneath my fingers. The ground spun. I was going to fall.

But before I did, Shana was there, her hands on my legs. Her cold fingers circled my ankle, and she gave me a comforting squeeze. A second later, her gravelly voice rose above the music.

"You're okay," she called. "One step down."

I nodded, and lowered my foot down a single rung.

She talked me down the ladder that way. I was too scared to climb back to the ground, so she stayed on the second-highest platform with me for hours. She sent people off to get me water and ice, and she held my hand and told dirty jokes until I felt sober enough to try the ladder again.

I down the rest of my water in one gulp. As terrifying as that night was, it was also exhilarating. We told the story for weeks afterward. Shana pushes me, but she protects me, too. We're a team.

"*Please.*" Shana flashes me her little-kid smile. I hate saying no to that smile.

"We don't even know where it is," I say instead. "You have to know somebody."

"Woody knows a guy."

Of course he does. On cue, Woody, the lead singer for Feelings Are Enough, pushes through the crowd, his forehead still slick with sweat from the bright stage lights. He runs a hand through his blond, surfer-dude hair and winks at the girl with the spiky green hair sitting next to me.

"Hey, Amy." His lips curl into a pouting half smile that he could only have learned from studying old posters of boy bands. He's wearing a cow costume zipped up to his waist—the arms and head flap around his legs. Pink plastic udders cover the front of his crotch.

"Did you wear that onstage?" I ask. Woody pretends to squirt me with an udder.

"Didn't you see me? I was standing right in front of you," he says, dropping the udder. "I had a Funky Chicken show earlier."

"You're still doing that?" I ask, wrinkling my nose. Funky Chicken is Woody's other band—a two-man rap group that performs in farm animal costumes and sings about chicken sandwiches and bongs.

"You kidding? We're blowing up. New video on YouTube every week." Woody does a little air guitar, twisting up his face like he's concentrating. "We were *on* tonight."

"We didn't suck." Sam walks up behind him and drops a hand on Woody's shoulder, and my heart nearly stops in my chest. "Hey," he says. "Nice hair."

I touch my newly buzzed hair, and a blush creeps over my cheeks. I picture brushing the sweaty strand of hair off Sam's face and burrowing my head into his T-shirt. I already know what he'd smell like: fabric softener and pine needles. I blink and look away. *Don't stare*, I tell myself, though I'm not sure my brain will register that

51

as a command. I can't *not* stare at Sam. It's as natural as breathing.

"Oh. Hey," I say, but he turns back around without another word. I bite back my disappointment. We dated for eight months and all he has to say to me is *nice hair*? I want to add something else, but what would be the point? My chest twists.

"Careful," Shana whispers. She leans behind me and slides the Tylenol bottle off the bar. My face flushes. I glance back at Sam to make sure he didn't see her. Before rehab, I used to hide oxy in old aspirin bottles so I could take them in public without anyone giving me a hard time. Sam found my stash once, and he was pissed.

Shana slips the bottle into her purse. The only thing inside is Tylenol, but Sam doesn't know that.

Thank you, I mouth to her. She winks at me.

Sam turns around. His eyes find mine then flick away. "So," he asks. "Are you guys going to this thing? Survive the Night?"

A thrill of adrenaline charges through my body. He might have asked both of us, but it felt like he was talking to me. Just like that, I make up my mind. This isn't just an illegal underground rave anymore. It's an illegal underground rave with my perfect ex-boyfriend who never should have dumped me.

I sneak a look at Shana, thinking of the possibilities. Another chance with Sam, maybe. A chance to make things right. "Yeah," I say, ignoring the heat climbing my neck. "I'm in."

FIVE

"GUYS!" AYA WOBBLES OVER TO A RICKETY wooden chair sitting in front of a dumpster. Her spiky heels dangle from one hand and black gunk stains the bottoms of her feet. Just looking at them makes me gag.

"She's going to get chlamydia of the foot," Julie says, twisting the onyx ring on her finger.

"Maybe we should buy her some flip-flops." I stare down at a bright blue gob of gum on the concrete. There are probably millions of diseases you could pick up on these sidewalks, but shopping's not really an option out here. We took the subway into Lower Manhattan, and it looks like a completely different city. The cute brick apartment buildings and tiny community parks have disappeared. Huge, empty office buildings stand in their place, their windows dark. They tower over us, cold and austere.

I wrinkle my nose and look away, dimly wondering how much longer we have to do this before officially giving up. It turns out the "guy Woody knows" was just someone he overheard talking back at the Cog. We've been searching for the secret entrance to Survive the Night for over an hour. That tingly, excited feeling I had when we left the Cog Factory has faded. This whole thing was supposed to be about talking to Sam, but the only thing Sam's said to me was "watch out" when I almost stepped in dog crap.

I sigh, and a strand of hair flutters away from my face. I can just make out Sam kneeling at the far end of the alley as he and Woody try to pry open a manhole cover. I should go over and help them, maybe even find a way to brush Sam's arm or lean against his shoulder. But the thought of making the first move turns my stomach.

I need to find a way to get his attention. I loop my arm through Julie's. "Are you still going to that SAT tutor?" I ask. "Craig something?"

"You mean Chris?" Julie scuffs the toe of her combat boot into the dirty concrete. The boots give her a good two inches of height, but her loose-fitting jeans still drag along the streets.

"Right," I say. Sam glances over his shoulder at us. Before we broke up, he was always saying I needed to focus more on college. I raise my voice. "*Chris*. Do you think he has room for one more student? I'm a little behind."

Shana stops at the industrial door to one of the warehouses and jiggles the handle. The loud, metallic rattle cuts me off. She's been doing this for the last twenty minutes, hoping someone left a door unlocked so we can sneak inside and explore.

Sam glances at her and shakes his head, then turns back to the manhole cover. Disappointment stabs through me.

"Give it up, Shana." I kick an empty Sprite can at her. It rattles across the alley and smacks into the door.

"Where's your sense of adventure?" Shana asks, jiggling another door handle.

"At home with my comfy shoes," I mutter, glaring down at my studded leather flats. They pinch my toes, and my feet ache from all the walking. A corner booth at IHOP and a stack of strawberry-banana pancakes is sounding pretty good about now.

"Guys, look!" Aya drops her shoes to the ground and scrambles onto the ledge of a dumpster, flashing us her bright pink panties. "Look! I'm so high."

I glance back over at Sam. He pulls at the manhole cover, grunting. I sigh, relieved that he isn't paying attention to my friends.

"How much did she have to drink?" I ask. Julie shrugs.

"I don't think she had anything. But I gave her one of these." She pulls a wrapped candy out of her pocket and hands it to me. It looks like a Jolly Rancher, except the wrapper is a plain, unmarked yellow.

"Great," I say, turning the candy over. "What's in it?"

"Nothing. Just a little pot." Julie takes the candy back from me, unwraps it, and pops it into her mouth. "Barely any. Aya can't handle her drugs."

Aya stands, spreading her arms out to either side. Her hair falls loose from her chignon, and her cardigan slips off one shoulder. She wobbles on the edge, too close to falling inside with the rotting garbage.

"Let me help you down, sweetie." I grab her legs to hold her steady. She blinks, like she can't quite remember where she is, and takes my hand, half stepping, half falling into my arms. I groan beneath her weight.

Shana jiggles another door handle. This one creaks open.

"Oh my God!" She pushes the door all the way open and steps into the warehouse. "Score!"

"Shana, don't." I stare into the darkness behind her. "You don't know what's in there."

"Exactly," Shana says. "And if you don't come after me, I could *die*."

She wraps her hands around her neck and sticks out her tongue, backing into the warehouse. She leaves the door open behind her.

Sam says something to Woody, and the two of them head farther down the alley. *Great*. I watch him walk away, then glance back at the warehouse door.

"Shana!" I call. Aya starts giggling and tries to climb back onto the Dumpster. My friends seem to be competing over who can embarrass me the most tonight.

"You, *sit*," I tell Aya, pointing at the ground. "Julie, help her get her shoes back on. I'm going to get Shana."

Then, before either of them can argue, I hurry across the alley and step into the warehouse. Crumpled up magazines and empty McDonald's containers litter the floor. Silver light slips through the cracks in the cardboard taped over the windows.

I hesitate at the door, reluctant to move farther inside.

"*Shana*," I hiss. It's too dark to see anything but hulking shadows. A crowbar leans against the wall just inside the door. I grab it and hold it in front of me like a weapon. The cold metal bites into my palms. I take a tentative step inside.

For some reason, I'm reminded of Mountainside. After Rachel died, I got a new roommate, this girl named Tanya. Tanya was a sleepwalker. A couple of times a week she'd creep out of bed and disappear into the clinic. The nurses told me I didn't have to look for her, but I couldn't help it, not after what had happened to Rachel. I couldn't sleep if I didn't know where Tanya was. I'd lie in bed, picturing all the different ways she could die.

At night, Mountainside was a chilling place. The floorboards creaked and shadows stretched across the long, narrow halls. And then there was the screaming. Withdrawal is worst during the night. Girls would sob and mutter to themselves and scratch at their doors. The sounds echoed around me as I crept past their dorms, calling Tanya's name.

I blink and my eyes start to adjust. I'm not at Mountainside—I'm in a gross warehouse with Shana. A bare mattress lies in the corner, a large black stain spread across its surface. I look away.

"Just dirt," I mutter under my breath, knowing that's not true. I move farther into the warehouse, tightening my grip on the crowbar. Nerves climb the backs of my legs, making my knees feel weak.

Something flickers at the corner of my eye. I whirl around, swinging the crowbar. A cat leaps from the windowsill to the floor, its paws silent on the concrete. Thick yellow pus oozes from a wound on its side and clumps in its fur.

My stomach churns. The cat watches me with glassy eyes.

"Damn it," I whisper. I move deeper into the warehouse, careful to step around the trash littering the floor. I listen for movement or for Shana's familiar throaty laugh. But I only hear my own ragged breath. The crowbar nearly slips from my sweaty hands.

The space is smaller than I expected, just one room about the size of a garage. A second door stands ajar at the side wall, sending a sliver of light through the darkness.

Something shuffles through the trash next to me. Every muscle in my body tightens. I spin around.

"Shana?" I whisper. I hold my breath and raise the crowbar. No one answers. I step forward, wiping a sweaty hand on my jeans. Dimly, I remember the screams echoing through Mountainside. Goose bumps rise on my arms.

A crumpled-up piece of newspaper rustles. I wrap my fingers around the crowbar again. "Shana? Is that you?"

A second cat appears beneath the newspaper and darts for the door.

I breathe a sigh of relief. To hell with this place. Shana can live here, for all I care. I lower the crowbar and edge around a pile of blankets.

The blankets move, and an arm shoots out and grabs my ankle. I scream, and whip my crowbar around. It slips from my hands and clatters to the floor.

A man with a cracked, ashen face peers out from the nest of blankets. He's missing an eye, and the skin over the socket looks shiny and raw. It grows mottled around his cheekbone and forehead. Flaps of puckered, black-ened flesh jut off his face.

Fear grips my chest. My heart thuds, and I can't seem to find my voice. I feel like I'm in a dream where I want to scream but I can't. Except this isn't a dream. I glance over at the crowbar, but it's too far for me to reach.

"Your friend went that way," the man says in a gravelly voice, nodding at the door. He lets go of my leg and burrows back under the blankets.

I run for the door.

I burst into the cool night air and there's Shana leaning against the alley wall. She takes a puff of her cigarette and blows the smoke out through her teeth. Another homeless man stands next to her. Dirt and grease line his face, but he's younger than the one-eyed man I saw inside. Thick blond dreadlocks hang down his back, and he has plastic grocery bags knotted around his feet instead of shoes.

The tension drains from my shoulders, but adrenaline still pounds through my veins, leaving me hot and jittery. My heart beats like crazy. It's almost like being high.

"I'm going to kill you," I say, letting the warehouse door slam behind me. Shana flicks her cigarette, sending a shower of ash to the ground.

"Then why are you smiling?" she asks. I bite my lip. It's that giddy thing again. I can't get scared without grinning like an idiot.

Besides, the warehouse was kind of exciting. In a terrifying way.

"I want you to meet my new friend," Shana says. "Casey, this is Lawrence."

The homeless man flashes me a peace sign, quietly humming under his breath. Shana passes him her cigarette, and he takes a deep drag.

"Um, hi," I say. Lawrence tries to hand the cigarette back to Shana, but she waves him away.

"Keep it," she says. "Case, you'll never guess what Lawrence just told me."

I raise an eyebrow, waiting.

"Lawrence was telling me about this alley a couple of blocks over." Shana stands on one foot, scratching the back of her leg with her boot. "Get this. The alley was singing."

"*Humming*," Lawrence interrupts, his voice deep and melodic. He takes another puff of Shana's cigarette. "The alley was humming, not singing. There weren't any words."

"That's right," Shana says. "Don't you think that's crazy, Casey? A humming alley?"

"Humming?" I repeat. Shana gives me a comically slow, intentional wink and something clicks inside my head. "Wait, you mean there was music playing? Under the alley?"

Lawrence frowns. "I guess it could have been music," he says.

I jog to the corner and peer down the opposite alley. Woody crouches in the middle of the street, his head pressed against a manhole cover. The cow costume still hangs from his waist, looking worn. Dirt and grease stain the limp tail and the cow's white ears.

"I don't think this is it," he mutters.

Sam stands over him, frowning. "I'm telling you, he said *Covert* Street, not Cooper Street," he says.

"Maybe." Woody pushes himself to his feet and heads farther down the alley. He kicks a beer can, and it skitters behind a Dumpster.

"Guys!" I shout at them. "Shana found something."

Sam and Woody jog over to us, Aya and Julie trailing behind them. Aya's only wearing one of her shoes and carrying the other. She loses her balance when she tries to walk and stumbles into Julie, giggling.

"What's up?" Sam asks. Woody stares at Lawrence's grocery bag shoes as Shana repeats the story of the humming alley.

Woody pulls his wallet out of his back pocket and removes a twenty-dollar bill. "Lawrence, my man, how'd you like to make some money?" he asks.

Lawrence leads us through the darkened Manhattan streets, to another alley several blocks over. Woody walks beside him, but Sam lags behind. Now is my chance. I fumble with my turtle necklace and hurry up next to him.

"Hey," I say, nudging him on the shoulder.

"Hey," he says back. Usually his voice is casual, and even a little cocky. Now it sounds strained. I roll my lower lip between my teeth, and silence stretches between us.

"So." I cough awkwardly. "Um, how's school?"

Sam shrugs. His jeans hang low on his hips and his shirt's a little wrinkled, like he dug it out of the back of his dresser. "Same," he says.

"Any news about James?" I ask. James is Sam's older brother. He was the one who taught Sam to play guitar, but he's a meth addict, and he disappeared right before graduating high school. He's been MIA for a little over a year. Because of him, Sam never touches drugs. He doesn't even drink.

Sam glances up at me. Some of the tightness leaves his jaw. "Nothing new," he says in a voice that sounds a little more like normal. "Heard he was in California, but who knows?"

Sympathy tugs at my chest. "He hasn't called?"

"Once." Sam pinches the bridge of his nose with two fingers. "It was weird. He didn't even sound like himself."

I rub my thumb over Myrtle's shell. Tori Anne, from Mountainside, was a meth addict. She spoke with a lisp because the drug had rotted all her teeth.

"I'm sorry," I say. Sam shakes his head.

"Don't be," he says. "You didn't do anything."

Woody calls Sam's name, and Sam jogs up next to him, leaving me alone. Shana nudges me with her arm.

"So cute," she says. I stare at the back of Sam's neck, where his hair brushes against his shirt collar.

"You never thought so before," I tell her. Back when we were dating, she used to call him "that little puppy who follows you around." She told me to find him a new home.

Shana winks at me. "Oh, yeah. The cow costume's a *total* turn-on," she says, and I realize she's talking about Woody. The jealousy I felt fades away.

"It's probably the udders," I say. Shana loops her arm through mine, and the two of us fall in line behind Julie and Aya.

"You should have seen how he looked at me," I whisper when the others are out of earshot. Shana frowns.

"Who? *Sam?*" she asks. I shoot her a look.

"Of course Sam."

"How did he look at you?"

I shrug, not sure how to explain it. I think of the tightness in his jaw, the strained sound of his voice.

"Like I'm broken," I say finally. Shana raises an eyebrow. "Like I remind him of James," I add.

Shana brushes the hair back from my face and kisses my forehead. "You're nothing like James," she says.

"You weren't there," I say. My voice cracks, and I have to stop and take a breath. I don't want to cry in front of Shana, not with Sam just a few feet away, but I don't know how to talk about Mountainside without bringing up all these weird emotions. "Those girls in rehab," I continue. "They were—"

"Stop." Shana cuts me off. "They might have been broken, but that doesn't mean you are. You're stronger than that."

I don't answer right away. Her voice gets harder. "Do you understand?"

I sigh and nod, wanting to believe her. Ahead of us, Julie leans her head back, staring up at the sky. Dark curls trail down her back. She hums "Twinkle, Twinkle, Little Star" under her breath.

"*This* is where you belong," Shana adds. "With us. Tell me you didn't miss this."

"Wandering around New York in the middle of the night?" I ask.

"It's like *eleven*. Hardly the middle of the night. And I meant hanging with your friends. Going on an adventure." Shana elbows me. "Remember that night at the playground?"

I groan, thinking about the time Shana showed up in the middle of the night and woke me up by throwing pebbles at my window. She used to do that sometimes, when she and her mom had a fight and she needed to get out of the house to cool down. I had expected her to take me to some illicit party, but instead she drove to the playground two blocks away. She grabbed my arm and pulled me over to the swing set.

"Race you," she said, plopping down a swing.

"To where?" I asked.

Shana shrugged. "The moon."

Shana swung higher and higher, pumping her legs until the chains groaned and the swing set lurched in place. Then—when she was so high it looked like she'd tip over and fall backward—she jumped.

She fractured her ankle in three places. I had to carry her back to the Buick and drive her to the hospital. I called her mom at least seven times, but she never even picked up the phone. My mom answered on the first ring.

"I'd prefer not to end up in the emergency room tonight," I say, leaning my head on Shana's shoulder. "Maybe this adventure can end with food?"

"Man cannot live on bread alone, Casey," she says.

"What about pancakes? I'm pretty sure man can live on pancakes."

A rat scurries across the alley, its pink tail whipping behind it. It freezes in the middle of the street and stares at us with red eyes.

"Holy shit!" I take a quick step back.

Aya screams and stumbles over her feet. Julie bursts out laughing but grabs Aya's arm so she doesn't fall. The rat twitches its nose. I flinch. I imagine it darting toward us, snapping its long, sharp teeth. But it creeps along the curb and out of sight instead. I sigh in relief.

Shana takes a swig of Jack Daniel's. "It's just a rat, guys," she says, tucking the bottle back into her pocket.

"It's disgusting," Aya mutters. Julie kicks a soda can into the shadows where the rat disappeared, and something darts across the pavement. Aya releases another high-pitched shriek, and Julie laughs even harder.

Suddenly, Lawrence stops walking. He, Sam, and Woody crouch down in the street.

"This is it!" Woody shouts, wiping the dirt off a manhole cover. The rest of us crowd around him.

"Feel that?" Lawrence asks. Music vibrates through the ground, making the street hum.

"Cool," I say, crouching next to Sam. I'm close enough that I can smell him, the combination of soap and pine needles.

The manhole cover's made of iron, with a City of New York logo stamped over the center. Someone has painted a neon pink X over it. Woody digs his fingers around the sides of the cover and yanks.

"Are you sure that's the right . . ." Julie starts, but she lets the end of her sentence trail off when Woody grunts and shoves the cover to the side of the hole.

"X marks the spot," he says, wiping his hands off on his costume. Shana grabs my arm and jumps up and down, squealing. Together, we all peer into the darkness.

A rickety metal ladder descends into the black. Far below, I can just make out flickering candlelight and hear the distant sound of drumming. Something drips against the bottom of the tunnel, and the sound echoes toward us.

"Well," Sam says, leaning back on his heels. "Who wants to go first?"

SIX

I LOWER MYSELF DOWN THE LADDER. THE RUNGS chill my fingers even though the day's heat still lingers in the air.

"Gross," I say. "It smells like fish."

"It's an adventure." Julie climbs onto the ladder above me. Her Doc Martens combat boots clank on the rungs, making the entire ladder tremble. She got the boots from her mom, who was way into grunge in the nineties and had written *Pearl Jam rules* across the leather in silver Sharpie. "Adventures aren't supposed to be clean."

"That's the weirdest thing you've ever said," Aya mutters. She crawls into the opening next, carefully placing one blackened foot onto the ladder's rungs.

"You didn't care about being smelly when you were

playing Queen of Garbage earlier," I say. Julie pokes Aya's foot and snickers.

Aya tries to kick her. "Hey, stop shaking the ladder," she says. A nervous laugh bubbles up in my throat. We're kind of high up, and this thing doesn't exactly feel steady. I glance down, but I can't see past Shana's blond head. My leather flat slips from my heel, and I curl my toes to keep it from falling.

"Don't tell me you're scared." Shana's voice echoes up from below me. I tighten my grip on the ladder rungs, feeling dizzy.

"I never get scared," I shoot back. Something icy and cold slithers down the back of my shirt. I shriek, nearly losing my grip on the ladder. My shoe slips off my foot and spirals into the darkness.

Shana cackles. "Yeah, you're a badass."

I rock back and forth to make the ladder jiggle. Shana screams with laughter and hugs herself to the rungs.

"Shit!" she shouts. "I take it back. Don't do that again."

I laugh as we climb deeper underground and the subway tunnel slowly comes into focus. A giant laughing clown face stretches across one wall, orange spray paint dripping down the tile. Candles flicker on the ground. Distant music echoes through the tunnel and pulses up from the floor, making the wicks tremble.

Excitement floods through me. I can already hear voices and laughter coming from deeper in the tunnel. It sounds like the party's in full swing. I lower my foot and my toes hit wet concrete. Chills shoot up my leg.

"Ewww." I giggle, balancing on one foot. We've reached a narrow platform overlooking a single row of grimy train tracks. A water-stained poster reads SERVICE CHANGES. I flatten the edge of the paper, but it's too faded to read.

"That's hella old," Woody explains, stepping up behind me. "These tunnels have been closed since Hurricane Sandy."

"Creepy," I say, and another thrill of excitement shoots through me. I turn, still balanced on one foot. "Has anyone seen my shoe?"

"This it?" Sam holds up my shoe, turning it so the candlelight catches the studs on the toe. Even in the dark I see the little dimple in his cheek.

"Yeah," I say. I clear my throat, annoyed at how breathless and girlie I sound.

"Catch!" He tosses me the shoe and I awkwardly lunge to catch it.

"Thanks," I say, slipping my shoe back on. Sam gives me a thumbs-up. I'm not entirely sure how to respond to a *thumbs-up* from the only boy I've ever loved, so I just nod.

"Aw, it's like an incredibly awkward Cinderella," Shana says. She pulls another cigarette out of the pack of Djarum Blacks that she steals from her corner market, and strikes a match. The blue-orange flame flickers over her pale skin and pink-tipped hair. Silvery smoke snakes around her.

"Does that make you my evil stepsister?" I say, once Sam's too far away to hear.

"Are you kidding? I'm your fairy godmother." Shana winks and taps her cigarette, sending a shower of orange sparks to the ground.

"What does that mean?" I ask.

"You'll see." She squeezes my shoulder, then hurries up to walk with Woody and Sam. I lag behind, turning the comment over in my head. Shana is like a firecracker: bright and sparkly and fun—but if you set her off in the wrong direction, she'll light everything on fire.

The platform stretches for another hundred feet before ending at a white-and-green-tiled wall. A staircase cuts through the middle of the concrete, leading deeper underground.

"Where now?" I ask, peering down the stairs. Particleboard and two-by-fours seal off the door below, and caution tape winds around the handrails. This place is a freaking maze. I wonder how deep it goes.

Woody hops off the platform, motioning for us to follow him down onto the tracks. Sam climbs down next. I hesitate, looking at Julie, Aya, and Shana.

"Let's do this," Shana says, jumping into the tunnel. Three rusty train rails cut down the center, surrounded by red Solo cups, empty PBR cans, and Snickers wrappers.

Rows of thick white candles line the walls. The steady *bomp bomp bomp* of techno music echoes toward us. I can't help bouncing a little as I walk. I want to *dance*.

"Is it true what they say about the third rail?" Aya asks, hopping down next to me.

"You mean, is it electrified?" Woody picks up a plastic cup and tosses it at the far rail. It rolls away, unharmed.

"They turned the power off, remember?" Julie says. "Because of the hurricane?"

"Whatever." Woody kicks another plastic cup at the rail.

I wrap my arms around my chest, shivering. Party sounds seep up through the floor and ooze out of the walls, reverberating through the soles of my shoes. The ground trembles with music.

We turn the corner, and the tunnel opens into an underground station with an arched ceiling and graffiti-covered walls. People crowd on top of a concrete platform, waving yellow and pink glow sticks that leave trails of light as they dance. Two lanes of subway tracks stretch past the platform on both sides before disappearing into dark tunnels just like the one we've come out of. Strobe lights flash from the ceiling, and hundreds of candles line the walls, dripping pools of white wax.

"Whoa." Julie runs a hand through her hair, sweeping the black curls off her face. "It's like Christmas. But for ravers."

"Ravemas," Aya adds, giggling. She tugs off her cardigan,

revealing the plunging neckline on her fifties-style dress. She folds the sweater into a tiny square and forces it into her pink faux-fur clutch. She wobbles toward the party, once again balancing on her painful-looking heels.

"How long before she finds the newest love of her life?" Julie asks, twisting the onyx ring on her finger.

"Maybe she'll find someone great tonight," I say. Aya's always looking for her next epic romance. Julie gives her shit, but I can't help rooting for her. I steal a glance at Sam, heading down the tunnel.

"You think there's a VIP room in this place?" Shana asks, taking a puff from her cigarette.

"Like where the celebs hang out?" I ask. Shana shrugs and leans her head back, trying to blow smoke circles.

"This *is* New York," she says, winking at me.

I lean forward, peering down the tunnel that leads to the entrance. "Maybe it's back this way?"

I start down the tunnel, but a bouncer cuts me off before I can go any farther. He has the kind of face that looks like it doesn't know how to smile.

"No one leaves Survive the Night until the party's over," the bouncer says. He hooks his thumbs into his jeans pockets and stands up straighter. He must be more than six feet tall.

I glance at Shana, "We're just looking for . . ."

"A bathroom," she finishes for me.

"Party's not over till five," the bouncer says.

"Come on," Shana says, pulling me back into the party.

"That was weird," I say. "We're trapped down here until five in the morning. Don't you think that's—"

"Cool?" Shana stomps out her cigarette.

"I was going to say strange." I check over my shoulder again. The bouncer leans against the wall next to the tunnel, waiting for anyone else who might try to slip back to the entrance. "Shana, we have to drive back before Madison's sleepover gets out or my parents will know I bailed."

"It takes two hours to get back," Shana says. "You'll be fine."

"But if there's traffic . . ."

"At five in the morning?" Shana picks at the nail polish on her thumb. "I'm going to find us something to drink," she says, letting a black flake flutter to the ground. "Think you can try to relax until I get back?"

"Yeah, of course," I say, a little embarrassed that I'm getting so worked up.

Shana veers off to the drink line, while I scramble onto the platform to look for Julie and Aya. Narrow ledges jut out from the wall above me. A girl with pigtails sits on one of them, spray-painting a face on the concrete. I ease past a group of people playing Spin the Bottle and try to make my way toward the dancers on the far end. The platform's so crowded I can barely move. I'm about to give up and follow Shana to the drink line when I stumble over a pair of Converse sneakers and balled-up socks.

"Left foot, green!" someone shouts.

I push past a line of people and see another, smaller group. It looks like they're wrestling. Paint coats their hands and feet and drips from their clothes. Messy puddles of red, yellow, blue, and green cover the concrete and ooze together, making the floor look like a Jackson Pollock painting.

"Right hand, blue!"

Everyone scrambles around to find the blue paint puddles. Giggles erupt as their hands slip out from under them. A few people lose their balance and fall.

I grin as I watch them play, thinking back to the party where I met Sam. I kept waiting for him to come inside so I could make an excuse to talk to him, but he spent most of the night in the yard with his lawn mower.

Then, about halfway through the party, I saw him slip through the front door and sneak upstairs. I found him alone in an office on the second floor.

"I was looking for an extra bathroom," he told me. But when I promised I wouldn't rat him out, he admitted he was actually snooping.

"Check this out," he'd said. He stepped aside, revealing a floor-to-ceiling bookcase completely stocked with old board games. They had everything: Jenga, Trivial Pursuit, Life, Monopoly, Sorry!—you name it. My mouth dropped open when I saw it—I didn't realize people owned board games anymore. I hadn't seen so many in one place in my entire life.

I threw a hand over my eyes. "Whatever game I point to is the one we're going to play," I'd said. He laughed while I made a big show of waving my hand over the row of games before dropping it on an old Twister box.

"I don't think you can manage Twister," Sam said, nodding at the bulky knee brace I had to wear after my accident.

"Rain check," I'd told him. He found a piece of paper and scribbled *IOU one game of Twister* on it, along with his phone number.

I can't help remembering that moment now, as I watch this much messier game of Twister. I swivel around, trying to find Sam in the crowd. I know things have been weird between us, but an IOU is an IOU. He owes me a game.

"Right foot, blue," the announcer shouts. I grin as the players weave and duck around one another and people lose their balance and tumble to the floor. I finally spot Sam a few feet away. He slides his bare foot onto a blue puddle, a streak of red paint smudged across his face.

The smile freezes on my lips. He's already playing. Without me.

The announcer shouts something else, but his voice sounds like static. A girl leans over and whispers something in Sam's ear. She's beautiful and blond, and wearing a shirt that's so short and tight it's practically nonexistent. Sam laughs and touches her bare shoulder. The hurt burns inside me, turning to fury.

I push through the crowd to get to the game, shedding my shoes as I go. Sam freezes when he sees me, his hand hovering above a goopy blue pile of paint.

"Oh, hey," I say, flashing him my sexiest smile. "I didn't see you playing."

The blond girl glares at me, and I very maturely stick out my tongue when Sam turns his head.

"Right hand, green," the announcer calls. Sam slides his hand onto the same green blob I'm aiming for, and his thumb brushes against mine. I glance up at him. A blush colors his cheeks, and he jerks his hand away.

"Sorry," he mutters. I grin, and flick a little red paint at him. It splatters across his hair.

"Sorry!" I say, biting my lip to keep from laughing.

Sam cocks an eyebrow. "You're going *down*," he says, wiping paint from his face.

"Left food, red!" the announcer shouts. I plop my foot down, and red paint oozes between my toes. It feels cold and slimy. I try not to make a face, but I can't help scrunching my nose up in disgust.

"Ewww," I say. Sam lowers his foot to a red puddle behind me.

"Left hand, yellow!"

The blond girl hip-checks me, nearly sending me down. My knee twists, and pain flutters through my leg. Sam grabs my shoulder to hold me up. I regain my balance, and he pulls his hand back.

"Right foot, red!"

This time, Sam starts to stumble. He grabs my shoulder for support, and suddenly, we're practically nose-to-nose.

"Hey," he says. "You have a little . . ." He brushes something off my cheek. I hold my breath. A smile flickers onto his lips.

"So, I was trying to wipe away a dot of yellow paint," he explains, "and I accidentally smeared green paint all over your face."

"Loser!" I push my hand into his face, leaving a bright blue handprint on his cheek. He laughs and dunks his hand back down in the red paint. I dodge backward, but I lose my balance. I grab Sam's sweatshirt, pulling him into the paint with me. I hit the ground with a thud, and Sam lands on top of me.

"You and you!" the announcer calls, pointing to us. "You're out."

"We're out," Sam says. He pushes himself onto his elbow, but doesn't move right away. Instead, he stares down at me. My breath catches. He's so close. He could kiss me. I want him to kiss me.

Finally, he clears his throat and pushes himself away. He reaches for my hand to help me up.

"Good game," he says with a smile.

SEVEN

SAM PULLS ME TO MY FEET. "WE'RE A MESS," HE says.

I try to laugh, but it sounds hollow. Blue paint drips from Sam's T-shirt and stains his jeans. I lift my hand to wipe a smudge of yellow off his chin, but Sam clears his throat and looks over his shoulder before I can touch him. Frowning, I let my arm drop back to my side.

I glance down at myself instead. Red and green hand-prints cover my black T-shirt and jeans, and there's blue paint splattered over my feet.

"Think there's somewhere we can clean up?" Sam asks.

"Don't think you're going to find a bathroom down here." I wipe my paint-covered hands on my jeans, but there's nothing I can do about my feet. I slip them into my flats, leaving blue smudges on the leather.

"Come on," Sam says, nodding at a keg sitting in the corner. "Let's find something to drink."

I hesitate. "Beer's probably not a good idea. For me, at least."

"Water, then." A real smile crosses his face, crinkling the corners of his eyes. It's enough to calm the butterflies in my gut.

Sam grabs his sneakers and takes my hand, pulling me into the crowd. His skin feels chalky from the dried paint, and a little sweaty. I don't want him to let go, but he releases his grip when we shuffle to the end of the drinks line.

"Isn't that Shana?" he says, nodding at a blond head in the crowd around the keg. I cup my hands around my mouth.

"Shana!" I call, and she whips around, holding two bright red Solo cups.

"Hey! I was looking for you two," she says. She hands me a Solo cup. "It's *soda*," she says when I make a face. "Don't get your panties in a twist."

"Yum," I say, taking a sip. "This is perfect. Thanks."

Shana shifts her eyes to Sam. "Woody was looking for you," she says. "He found some guys who want to jam. You in?"

Sam glances at me. "I didn't bring my guitar."

"They had stuff," Shana says.

"Uh, sure." Sam crosses his arms over his chest. "You coming?" he asks. He stares at my chin instead of meeting my eyes.

"Yeah." I bite my lip to keep from frowning. Shana grabs Sam's arm.

"Here, let me show you where they're all set up," she says, and pulls him into the crowd.

"Wait, didn't you want a drink?" I shout. Sam turns and lifts a hand to his ear, frowning.

"Didn't you . . ." I start again, but he shakes his head to show that he can't hear me over the music. "Never mind," I mutter, tagging along after them.

We hop off the platform and follow the tunnels deeper underground. Shana balances on one of the thick rails, holding her arms out to either side.

"Why don't people run off to join the circus anymore?" She wobbles but catches herself before she loses her balance. Beer sloshes over the rim of her Solo cup. "I'd be insane on the tightrope."

"You just want an excuse to wear a sparkly leotard." I avert my eyes as we walk past a couple making out by the side of the tracks. Shana spins on her rail.

"I'd look great in a leotard," she says. She wobbles again. I grab for her arm, but Sam reaches her first. He holds her elbow until she regains her balance.

I grit my teeth and kick an empty PBR can. It ricochets off a rusted rail and rolls to a stop in front of a silver subway car. Graffiti covers the windows, making it impossible to see inside. Woody's voice echoes down the tunnel, screeching the words to a popular Feelings Are Enough song.

Sam pulls himself onto the platform, then leans over to offer me a hand.

"Thanks," I say, hopping up next to him. A dull ache shoots through my knee. I wince and scramble to my feet, trying to stretch my leg as we walk.

We join a line of people trying to push through the narrow subway car door. The car's tiny, but a hundred people are jammed inside. Orange and pink glow-in-the-dark necklaces glimmer from their necks and wrists, and they wave glow sticks above their heads. A thick cloud of marijuana smoke gathers at the top of the subway car.

"Are you ready for some music?" Woody yells. If I squint, I can see him standing on a cracked yellow seat in the middle of the car. A faded subway map stretches across the wall behind him.

Woody's gone full cow, with the costume zipped over his chest and a plastic nose strapped over his real one. A black-and-white tail swings between his legs, and he has fifteen glowy pink necklaces dangling from his neck.

The crowd cheers. I spot Aya wrapped around a silver pole in the middle of the car, pumping her fists in the air. Wispy black strands of hair hang in front of her face. I search for Julie's bushy curls, but I don't see her.

"Come on," Shana shouts over the cheering.

She and Sam duck through the wall of people and disappear into the smoky car. I try to follow, but another jab of pain shoots through my knee. Grimacing, I step out of the doorway and lean against a graffiti-covered window.

I squint through the glass, watching Sam wade through the crowd and crawl onto the seat next to Woody. Someone hands him a guitar and he ducks his head to play.

Disappointment rolls through me. I thought I felt something shift when we were playing Twister, but Sam doesn't even scan the crowd to see if I'm watching.

I sigh and make my way farther down the platform to look for Julie instead. I refuse to be the girl who hangs around her ex-boyfriend when he obviously doesn't want her there. It's better that I give him a chance to miss me.

Julie's thick curls usually make her pretty easy to find, but it's so crowded down here that I can barely see two feet in front of me. I push my way through the partiers, wondering if she found a bathroom to hide in, like she did the night she came with Shana and me to the rave at the pool. She spent the entire night huddled in the back of the handicapped stall.

"Learn the secrets of your future, only a nickel," she had said when Shana and I finally came to find her. A lit joint was balanced on her knee.

I dug a nickel out of my pocket and handed it to her.

"Your aura's yellow," she said, sliding the nickel into her combat boot. "It means you're cheerful and good-natured but easily led astray."

"That's not the future," I pointed out. Julie picked up her joint with two fingers.

"Your good nature will lead you to love," she said. "And love will lead you to danger."

A toilet flushed, and Shana threw open her stall door. The hard plastic slapped against the wall.

"You're cracked, Jules," she said, switching on a faucet. "Sam's a Boy Scout. No danger there."

Julie leveled her eyes at Shana. She took a puff off her joint, and smoke curled up toward the ceiling.

"There are many different kinds of love," she said.

Techno music blasts from a set of wireless speakers, sending a deep *oontz oontz* trembling through the ground. I think I see someone with dark, bushy hair, and I grab her arm. But when she turns around I see that it's really a *he*, and his hair is actually a fake-looking wig.

"You're pretty!" someone shouts. I turn, and a skeletally thin boy wearing Goth makeup grabs my hand and pulls me into the crowd.

"Whoa," I say, stumbling after him. He yanks me toward a thick group of gyrating people and grabs my hips. For a second, I consider dancing with him. I even sneak a glance over my shoulder to see whether Sam's watching through the subway car window. Then I realize what I'm doing and pull away, disgusted with myself.

"No thanks," I say, untangling myself from Goth Boy's

arms. I am not that desperate. I take another drink of soda. It's warm now, but the air is so muggy down here that I don't mind. Everyone's sticky and sweaty and way, way too close. A sparkler crackles to life a few feet away, and people around me whoop and cheer. I wince, imagining a spark landing on my bare arm.

I duck away before someone else can force me to dance. The crowd thins out farther down the platform. I move around a boarded-off staircase and crouch beside the subway car to catch my breath. Candles sit along the steps in front of me, held in place with pools of sticky wax. I lean against the cool metal subway car and take another swig of soda, wishing I'd asked Shana for a little whiskey. At least then I'd be having fun.

Someone sniffles, quietly at first, and then louder. It almost sounds like a sob. I stand and peek into the subway car behind me. It's so dark that it takes a second for my eyes to adjust to the light.

Two kids huddle against the far door, looking down at something in their hands. I squint and move closer.

A lighter sparks. The flame illuminates a kid with long, stringy hair. White powder crackles from the spoon he holds with trembling fingers.

Shock roots my feet to the ground. Smoke floats lazily toward the top of the subway car.

I curl my fingers around the subway door and inhale the sweet, smoky scent. Everything in me wants to crawl into that tiny car and breathe in, deep. I can almost feel the drugs clouding my brain. I stumble back so quickly that I slam into the staircase. Smoke drifts toward me, beckoning. I clench my eyes shut, my head throbbing. I fumble for my purse, then freeze, remembering that Shana took my Tylenol.

Suddenly the dancing and cheering feels like an assault. The air in these tunnels is too thin. I gulp down mouthful after mouthful and still feel like I can't breathe. A dull ache flickers through my skull. I grit my teeth together and press my fingers against my temples. I stumble forward, and Goth Boy's there again, grabbing for my arm.

"Hey, beautiful," he starts. I pull away, trying to move around him, but I stumble and then I'm next to the wall, my face pressed against the smooth, cold bricks. Lights and colors and music pound around me.

"Hey," Goth Boy says. "Are you okay?"

"Water . . ." I murmur. The ground lurches beneath me. I stumble, smacking my shoulder against the wall. I try to push myself away from the wall, but the tile is warm to the touch, and the heat seeps into my fingers. I can't move my hand. It feels like I've plunged it into a pool of tar.

Goth Boy disappears, but I don't know whether he's really going to get me water or not. Black spots appear before my eyes. I take another drink of soda, surprised to find the cup nearly empty.

I feel woozy. I want to sit down, but there's nowhere

to sit.

"Casey?" I blink several times, and then Shana is there. Thank God. Her pink hair looks even pinker, if that's possible, and it's so beautiful and so perfect that I want to bury my face in it. I reach for her, but she's too far away, and my fingers just close around air.

"Whoa. You don't look so good," Shana says. But she's smiling. Why is she smiling?

"I don't know what's happening . . ." I say. My words slide together. "I feel so . . ."

High, I think but don't say. I can't be high. The only drug I've had tonight is caffeine.

I'm your fairy godmother. I remember Shana puffing on her cigarette, a mischievous look in her eye. I glance down at my cup—the cup Shana gave me. The last sip of liquid rolls around on the bottom.

"What did you do?" I ask. I blink, and my cup splits into two. Shana giggles.

"I'm helping you relax," she says, clamping a hand down on my shoulder. "You should *thank* me."

The two cups merge back into one again, but it's too big now. I don't know how to hold it.

"You drugged me," I say. My voice sounds very far away.

Shana presses my bottle of Tylenol into my hand. My fingers curl around it automatically.

"You're welcome," she whispers.

EIGHT

SHANA VISITED ME EVERY DAY AFTER MY KNEE
surgery. My soccer friends were busy with practice and games
and I could hardly get out of bed. But Shana always brought
me a present: a packet of watermelon Pop Rocks, a trashy tab-
loid magazine, a bag filled with tiny rubber dinosaurs. She'd
hang out in my room for hours, watching terrible reality televi-
sion and making up dirty limericks to scribble onto my cast.

A week after I got home, Shana plucked the orange pill
bottle off my bedside table and rattled it at me.

"Can I have one of these?" she asked.

"Why?" I frowned down at the wooden letters sitting in
front of me. We were in the middle of a game of Scrabble.
"They're just pain meds."

Shana laughed and popped the bottle open, dumping
the white pills into her palm.

"They're not just for pain," she said, tossing two into her mouth. "They can be for fun, too."

"Shana." I reach for my friend's hand, but it vanishes, leaving me grasping at air. "What did you give me?"

"Let's call it your glass slipper." Shana's voice is in my ear, and then it's gone. *She's* gone. I turn and stumble forward, catching myself against the tunnel wall.

I want to go home. I picture myself burrowing into my bed and pulling my familiar blue-and-purple paisley-print blanket over my face. I can practically feel the pillow beneath my cheek. My eyes drift closed, and I lean against the wall of the tunnel, breathing deep.

Home is so far away. I feel the distance suddenly, like a great, cavernous space. I miss my blanket and my pillow so badly my chest aches. I wish I were in bed now. I wish I were far away from all of this.

I push myself away from the wall, trying to ignore the churning feeling in my stomach. The colors around me switch places, and a film of sweat gathers on my lower back, just above my jeans. I think I'm going to vomit. But I just double over, gasping for breath.

When I straighten again, it feels like every person in the party has taken several steps closer to me. The flashing strobe lights distort their faces. Their skin melts from their skulls, like Popsicles in the sun.

A blond girl wearing blue eye shadow turns to me, skin

dripping from her cheekbones. Her eye sockets sag, then cave in on themselves, tearing the rest of her face down into the depths of the black. I lurch forward, grasping for the girl's face, but my hands close only on air.

I inhale, trying to calm myself down, but the air tastes like fish and rot and something else, something sweet and familiar that makes me gag. I need to get out of here. The air's too thick. I can't breathe.

I stumble toward the tunnel we all came down together. I see the entrance and hurry toward it. But the bouncer steps out of the shadows, blocking my way. I blink up at him. His torso dwarfs my entire body. And his head . . . His head doesn't look human. Thick, dark hair covers his cheeks and sprouts from his eyebrows. Then the hair starts to *grow*. It comes in faster and faster, until it covers the man's entire face.

I narrow my eyes. It's not hair—it's *fur*. Small, dark eyes stare out from beneath the fur. They're predatory. Like a bear's.

"Oh my God," I whisper, trembling. A snout juts out from the man's face where his nose should be. He peels his lips back, displaying teeth the length of kitchen knives. He's becoming the bear.

"No one leaves," the bear says. Drool drips from his teeth. I cower, horrified, and tears form at the corners of my eyes.

I turn and race back to the party before skin starts

melting from the bear's face. Elbows jab into my sides, and voices echo around me. I almost walk into a girl with long, silky black hair and perfect skin.

"Don't be stupid," she's saying to her friend, a curvy girl with dark skin and a wild Afro of hair.

"No, it's completely true!" the girl with the Afro says. "Mark told me there's this homeless guy who lives in the tunnels, and he's murdering all the hipsters coming down to party."

"Let me guess, this killer has a hook for a hand? Ooh, and I bet he escaped from a mental hospital at the edge of town."

"I'm serious! Some guy disappeared during the last rave—it was on the news and everything. Mark said they hushed up the part about it being a murder, but he was *there*. They never found his body, either, so it's probably still down here. *Rotting*."

The girls drop their voices to continue talking, and I can't hear them over the roar of the crowd anymore. I press my hands over my ears and squeeze my eyes shut, wishing I could melt into the ground. Everything's too loud, too close.

Glow sticks blur through the darkness beyond my closed eyelids, and a strobe light flashes in the corner. The lights ooze and twist together, making my head spin.

I stumble past the subway platform and down the train tunnel. Only then do I open my eyes again. I'm alone.

Finally. I collapse against the cool brick wall and breathe in deep. That sweet smell still lingers in the air, just beneath the rot of the sewer.

I look around, trying to figure out exactly where I am. The floor rises and falls beneath me, like it's breathing. A line of candles twists down the shadowy tunnel. Their light flickers over old subway tracks and travels up the walls around me. I move deeper into the tunnel. Laughter and music still echo from the main party, making my head pound. I follow the tracks until the voices are just a murmur in the distance. Graffiti covers the bricks.

WE'RE WATCHING one message reads in spiky green paint. Another says YOU'RE NEXT.

My drug-addled brain twists these words, making them look alive. They creep and move over the bricks. I blink, and the words go still. I wrap my arms around my chest, shivering. I know they'll start moving again as soon as I close my eyes. They're waiting for me to look away.

And then, out of nowhere, I hear a thin, horrified scream.

I step away from the wall. "Hello?" My voice booms around me, but I'm not sure if it's because I'm shouting or if the word echoes inside my own head. I make my way farther down the tunnel.

The candle flames flicker, gently, even though there's no wind. I fumble in my bag for my phone but come up empty-handed. I swear under my breath.

The shadows move. I stiffen. Rusty train tracks stretch ahead of me, then disappear into the black. The walls start to close in, but then I look at them and they jerk back into place. Someone traced their initials into the dust coating the walls. MC+RW 4EVA. I press my hand against the cool tile to keep the walls from moving again.

Lawrence, the homeless guy who led us here, lurches out of the tunnel. I stumble back, horrified. I hadn't realized he followed us down here. His dreadlocks writhe around his shoulders, like snakes. One of them pulls away from his head and hisses at me.

"Lawrence," I say, but the word gets stuck in my mouth. Lawrence's brilliant blue eyes seem to glow in the dark. Were they always blue? I seem to remember him having brown eyes, like warm coffee.

He doesn't look at me as he walks down the tunnel, barefoot, the grocery bags tied to his feet long gone. I try, again, to find my voice. "Lawrence, I need to find . . ."

Lawrence walks into me like I'm not there. I stumble backward, hitting my elbow against the wall. Pain shoots up my arm.

"Watch it!" I say, but I'm so high it sounds more like "Waaaa . . ." Lawrence keeps walking. His dreadlocks lie still, but there appears to be something on his back. It's long and hooked, the edges serrated like a knife. I watch as it shudders beneath his shoulder blades, then disappears, leaving only a bloody wound behind.

"Oh, God," I whisper. My ankle twists beneath me, and then I'm on the ground, my cheek pressed against the damp, earth-covered concrete. My hand smacks into a lit candle, and it topples over, rolling deeper into the tunnel.

It comes to rest near a pale hand.

I scream. I push myself to my hands and knees and crawl backward. I expect the hand to grab at me and drag its fingernails across my face. I imagine the sharp points digging into my flesh.

But the hand stays still. Lifeless.

Dead. Someone's dead. *Some guy died during the last rave*, I think, remembering the conversation I overhead. They never found his body. It's down here somewhere. Rotting.

I close my eyes and horror floods through me. I open them again, and the hand is gone. The candle flickers quietly, illuminating the dirt floor of the subway tunnel. I stare into the darkness until my eyes water. But I don't see anything.

I blink, and the hand is back. A black onyx ring glitters from its finger.

"Julie?" I whisper. No answer. My arms tremble beneath me, barely able to hold my weight. I crawl toward the hand. The candle sparks, then flickers out, leaving me in the dark.

"Julie!" My voice cracks. I want to reach out and grab her hand to make sure it's still warm. Then I imagine it

flipping onto its palm and crawling toward me like a spider. I run my fingers over the ground in front of me, but I feel only dirt and cold metal train tracks.

I swing my bag off my shoulder and dig inside. The darkness presses in on me. Something brushes my arm, and I scream. My bag slips from my hands and hits the ground. I grab for it and thrust my hand inside. My fingers bump up against my plastic cell phone case. I pull the phone out and switch the screen on. Light blinds me. I cringe and blink, waiting for the spots to clear from my eyes.

My throat goes dry. I aim the light into the darkness.

Julie's dark curls shroud her face and crawl across the ground like vines. My fingers tremble. I don't want to see anything else, but my hand moves on its own, lowering the phone's beam to illuminate the rest of her body.

Dried blood stiffens the front of her flimsy tank top and jeans. Patches of the blood still look fresh, but the edges have hardened into a brown crust that flakes onto the ground and stains Julie's skin. Wet red pools line the area below her fingernails and gather around her knuckles.

Vomit rises in my throat. I shake so badly I can hardly hold my phone. I shift the light to Julie's stomach.

A gaping wound opens up in the space below her ribs. Bits of bone poke through her shirt, glowing white in the shadows. It looks, impossibly, like someone carved out the middle of her body.

Something shuffles, and I flinch, moving my phone to illuminate a huge brown rat. Its red eyes reflect the light. It holds the tip of Julie's finger in its tiny pink paws and gnaws on it with sharp white teeth.

NINE

I SCREAM FOR SO LONG MY THROAT BURNS. THE rat drops Julie's finger and scurries deeper into the dark.

"Julie?" I whisper, hoarse.

Julie doesn't move. Blood coats her arms and neck and forms a black pool beneath her head. Another rat creeps from the shadows and laps at the pool of blood.

I cringe and look away. Something glistening spills from the hole in Julie's stomach. *Intestines.* They slither toward me, twitching. They splatter my face with something hot and sticky.

I scream. My phone slips from my sweat-slicked fingers and clatters to the ground. The screen blinks off.

Panicked horror claws at my chest. I'm alone. In the dark.

"Julie," I call, my voice stronger now. I hold my breath,

waiting, but there's only silence. The tunnel stretches and collapses around me. I dig my fingers into the spaces between the bricks on the wall and fight the queasiness rising in my throat. "Julie, *please*."

I hear something in the darkness. A footstep.

Nerves prick my neck. I picture the ragged hole in Julie's chest. Bones poking through skin. Shredded flesh. Hot, sticky pools of blood.

Someone made that hole. Bile rises in my throat. Someone cut into my friend's body, and they didn't stop when her eyes went still. The carved out her insides like she was an animal. They gutted her.

Another footstep, closer this time.

My knees tremble, but I push myself to my feet and start to run. My shoes slap against the damp floor. Tears blur my eyes and roll down my cheeks. Pain stabs through my bad knee. I keeping running, pushing myself to move faster. Faster. My foot slams into the concrete and my knee twists beneath me. I hit the ground palms-first.

For a second I lie there, frozen. I feel Julie's blood drying on my face. The sharp, metallic scent clouds my head, making me dizzy. I hear footsteps below the sound of my breathing, getting closer.

I grit my teeth together and push myself back to my feet. I picture the joints in my bad knee like tissues, the fibers slowly separating every time my foot slams into the ground.

The party glows in the distance. People writhe and dance. Music rumbles toward me and vibrates through the tunnel. Neon pink and orange lights flicker in and out of the darkness.

I hobble closer, but the party drifts deeper into the tunnel, like a mirage. Cramps knit my side, and a dull ache pounds through my knee. I wrap my arms around myself and breathe, deep.

"Help," I gasp. The throbbing music swallows my voice. I try to call out again, but the word bubbles up in my throat. I double over against the side of the tunnel, gasping for breath.

Run, my brain screams. But my muscles burn, and my knees shake so badly I can barely hold myself upright. I squeeze my eyes shut and try to focus on breathing.

Marijuana smoke hangs heavy in the air around me. I inhale and feel a gurgling deep in my belly, like everything I've ever eaten is rolling around with all the Coke I drank and whatever terrible drug Shana slipped me. Spots flash before my eyes, so I squeeze them closed. The room spins.

And somewhere in the darkness behind me: footsteps getting closer, closer.

I push myself away from the wall and try to run. My knee gives out after two shaky steps, and my hands and knees slam into the concrete. Pain shudders through my body. I try to stand, but I stumble again, banging my bad knee against a train track. Pain blossoms in my leg. Acid gurgles in my belly and climbs up my throat.

I double over, heaving, and vomit up everything in my stomach.

Sweat lines the back of my neck. My throat feels raw, and my chest burns. I spit the last of the vomit from my mouth and straighten, smoothing the hair back from my face. Everything looks a bit clearer now. The party is closer than I realized. There are more people nearby.

I'm crouched in a narrow tunnel separated from the rest of the party by thick concrete pillars. A dingy tile wall stretches behind me. Blue mosaic tiles spell out the words SOUTH FERRY.

A girl weaves around a pillar and stumbles past me, sloshing beer onto the train tracks. Party sounds echo through the tunnel. People dance and laugh and cheer.

I wipe my mouth with my palm and cringe. My stomach feels like someone hollowed it out with an ice cream scooper. I listen for the footsteps, but I only hear the steady bass thudding through the music.

I breathe in, deep, and stare back down the tunnel I just raced out of. Thick red rails disappear into the darkness. Candlelight makes the shadows dance. I crouch down and peel a candle off the floor.

My heart thuds against my ribs. I hold the candle in front of me, illuminating the moldy brick walls and dirt-covered concrete.

Something cracks, like a twig breaking.

I freeze. Every nerve in my body screams.

"Julie?" I whisper.

Silence.

Then someone grabs my shoulders.

TEN

HANDS CLAMP DOWN ON MY SHOULDERS. I THRUST my elbow behind me on instinct, making contact with the soft, fleshy area right below my attacker's ribs. The candle slips from my hands and smacks onto the damp floor, flickering out.

Behind me, a groan. "Casey?"

"*Sam?*" I whirl around, searching the darkness for Sam's face. The strobe lights at the end of the tunnel flicker on and off, illuminating the tips of his hair and the hard edges of his jaw. "Oh my God!"

"It's okay." Sam straightens, still rubbing the spot where I hit him. "Who did you think I was? The bogeyman?"

My throat closes up. I think of the footsteps I heard echoing through the dark. The rat's gleaming eyes. Julie's pale, lifeless body.

"Julie." My voice cracks. I still feel her blood clinging to my skin. I swipe at my cheeks but my hands come away clean.

"What are you doing?" Sam grabs my wrist but I jerk away.

"I have to get it off," I hiss.

"Get what off?" Sam grabs me and holds me still. I try to pull away but his fingers tighten around my arms. "Casey, *stop*. There's nothing on your face."

"The blood." I gasp. "I feel it."

"There's no blood!"

Sam pulls his phone out of his back pocket and switches on the camera. My face reflects back at me from the screen. Yellow paint streaks across my forehead, and there's a smudge of dirt at my chin. But no blood.

"No," I murmur. I touch the phone with a shaking finger. "I *felt* the blood. I saw it!"

"Whose blood?"

"Julie's!" I pull away from Sam and stumble toward the tunnel. "She's down there. She's hurt. I think she's . . . dead."

Sam narrows his eyes. "Casey . . ."

"You have to believe me!" I hear the twinge of hysteria in my voice and slow down, letting my heartbeat steady. "She's down there. We have to help."

I peer into the darkness, trying to separate the walls and floor from the oily black. I take a tentative step forward.

Sam touches my shoulder. I flinch.

"Here." He holds out his cell phone, sending a dim beam of light over the curved tunnel walls and metal train tracks.

"We'll look together, okay?" Sam nudges me with his shoulder. I swallow, and creep down the tunnel, feeling along the wall to find my way. Sam keeps his hand on my arm. Heat radiates off his body, reminding me I'm not alone.

The cell phone light bounces ahead, illuminating empty beer cans and the rotten wooden slabs beneath the subway rails. Water stains trace grimy lines down the brick. Someone has spray-painted neon yellow Xs along the wall.

I stare into the darkness just beyond the dim light, listening. I hear my own feet shuffling down the tunnel and the heavier sound of Sam's sneakers beside me. Nothing else. Goose bumps climb up my arms. I can't shake the feeling that someone's hiding in the shadows. I keep expecting Sam's cell phone light to illuminate a face.

"I don't know," I say after a few minutes. "Maybe this isn't the same tunnel. Julie was right—"

I kick something, and it skitters across the ground. Sam hands me his phone. I crouch down, aiming the beam of light at the floor.

My cell phone lies on the ground next to the curved brick wall. A thin crack spreads along the plastic case, cutting across the Sharpie kitten Shana had drawn on it.

I stand up, turning the phone over in my hand. "Someone could have moved her," I say.

"There would've been blood," Sam points out.

I aim my phone over the ground. The packed dirt looks damp, but that could be from beer or urine. "It could've seeped into the ground," I say, halfheartedly. "It could've . . ."

"Casey," Sam says. Hearing my name dislodges something in my chest. I release a choked sob.

"It wasn't her," I whisper. Relief bubbles up in my throat. It wasn't real. Julie's okay. Julie's alive. That's all that matters.

"Of course it wasn't her," Sam says, his voice oddly flat. "You're high, Casey."

I frown up at him. "No. It's not like that."

Frown lines wrinkle Sam's forehead. "So you're saying you didn't take anything tonight?"

I stiffen. "Nothing," I say, too quickly.

"A few seconds ago you were convinced you saw one of your best friends lying dead in a tunnel."

Shame warms my face. I always blush when I'm lying, which Sam knows better than anyone.

"*I* didn't take anything," I say carefully. I stare down at my shoes because I'm too embarrassed to look Sam in the face. I swore to myself I'd never lie to him again and here I am, falling right back into old habits. It's like nothing changed.

I swallow, and force the next words out of my mouth. "But I think Shana slipped something in my drink. I don't know what it was."

Sam shakes his head. "Bullshit."

"It's the truth," I say, meeting his eyes.

"How can I believe that?" Sam shakes his head. "I can't even count how many times you lied when we were together."

"I know." My voice cracks. I don't know how much I lied to Sam, either. At the time it seemed easier than telling the truth. Sam never understood why anyone would be curious about drugs. He had seen them ruin his brother's life, and he was convinced they'd do the same to me.

But things are different now. *I'm* different.

"I'm not the same person," I explain. "Rehab . . ."

"You're *exactly* the same person!" Sam stares at me, his jaw clenched. "You're still hanging out with the same people. You're still doing the same things."

"It's different now. I swear—"

"And what's with the Tylenol?" Sam reaches into my purse and grabs the bottle. "I'm not blind. I saw Shana hide it."

"That's what you're pissed about? It's Tylenol!" I take the bottle from him and flip the cap off, dumping half the pills onto the ground. They ping against the train tracks and scatter over the dirt. "There. Gone. Happy now?"

Sam stares down at the tracks. His shoulders slump.

"I just want you to take this seriously," he says. "You're acting like you don't remember what happened."

"Of course I remember." I bite my lip, hoping it's not a lie. There's a lot I don't remember, in truth, but I couldn't forget the day Sam broke up with me if I tried.

He came over first thing in the morning, before I was even really awake. I'd gone to this terrible party with Shana the night before, and my head throbbed. I asked Sam to wait for me outside, and then I dug an oxycodone out of the aspirin bottle where I kept them hidden. I didn't want to get high or anything; I just wanted to take the edge off my hangover.

"Do you know what happened last night?" Sam asked when I joined him on our porch swing. I frowned, trying to sort through my fuzzy memories of the night before. I remembered Shana ditching me at a party. And something about a fight?

"Whatever happened, it's over now," I said, leaning into Sam for a kiss. He pulled away.

"I can't do this," he said. He couldn't even meet my eyes. "I think you need help, Case."

"Help?" I blinked at him, confused.

"I watched the same thing happen with my brother," he said. "I'm worried about you."

"What are you talking about?" I was nothing like James. James was a junkie. He dropped out of school and disappeared. He didn't even talk to his family anymore. I told

Sam that he was being paranoid. Because of his brother, he was seeing addiction everywhere.

"Then tell me the truth," Sam had said. He finally looked up at me, sorrow crinkling the corners of his eyes. "Are you on anything right now?"

I stared at him, trying to decide if I should lie. But when I didn't answer, Sam shook his head and left.

I replay that moment in my head, blinking furiously to keep from crying. I've gone over it a million times, wondering if I could have said or done something differently.

"I'd do anything to change what happened," I tell him.

Sam studies me, his eyes narrowed. "That's why I can't figure this out."

I frown, feeling like I missed something. "Figure what out?"

"Why you're still hanging with Shana."

For a second I don't know what to say. Shana didn't have anything to do with our breakup. She wasn't even there. He must be talking about the night before rehab, the one I don't remember. I roll my lower lip between my teeth, trying to think of what to say.

"Look, I know she makes mistakes sometimes, but Shana's been a good friend to me—"

"She makes mistakes?" Sam interrupts. "Casey, you just told me she *drugged* you."

"I know." My voice catches in my throat. I don't know how to explain to Sam that I can hate Shana and love her at the same time.

"Look, I don't expect you to understand," I say finally. "She practically saved my life after I screwed up my leg."

"That's bullshit," Sam says. "If it weren't for her you never would have gotten addicted to your painkillers in the first place."

Heat climbs my neck and spreads across my cheeks.

"Maybe," I admit. I think back to the Scrabble game where Shana first took some of my oxycodone. Before that it had never occurred to me to take them just for the thrill of it, even when I wasn't in pain. "But she's been there for me, too, and she's the only one in my life who isn't treating me like a freak right now." Shana's words echo through my head: *You're nothing like those girls.* "She knows I'm not a junkie," I say.

Sam frowns. "Is that what she's telling you? That you don't have a problem? That everything's okay? Because that's a lie, Casey. You're a completely different person when you hang out with her."

A tear forms at the corner of my eye. "That was harsh," I say.

I turn and start back down the tunnel without waiting for his response. I can't do this anymore. Every word out of Sam's mouth feels like a slap. The tear rolls down my cheek and I brush it away, angry with myself for caring so much.

"Wait," Sam calls after me. He takes my arm and turns me around so I'm facing him again. "I just want to make sure you're okay. Things were bad for a while there. You weren't *you* anymore. The girl I fell in love with was gone."

"I'm right here," I whisper. Silence stretches between us. Sam takes a step toward me and clears his throat.

"I know," he says.

I open my mouth, then close it again. "Sam," I start, my mind whirring with all the things I want to say. "I know things got out of control. I'm so . . ."

"You don't have to do that," Sam says, shaking his head. "I made mistakes, too. If I could do it over again, I'd do things different."

I hold my breath. "Different how?"

Sam brushes the tears from my cheeks with his thumb, sending a trail of fire across my skin. His cell phone light blinks off, leaving us alone in the dark.

"I want to trust you again." His voice sounds husky, like there's something caught in his throat.

"You can," I say. "I missed you."

Sam leans in closer. "I missed you, too," he whispers.

ELEVEN

SAM HOVERS IN FRONT OF ME. HE'S SO CLOSE THAT
I can see the freckles scattered across his tan cheeks and
smell the Herbal Essences shampoo he steals from his
little sister. I hold my breath, worried that if I move, this
might all disappear.

Sam clears his throat. "We should probably go find the
others," he says.

"Yeah," I say.

He still doesn't move. I feel the seconds tick past. Sam
closes his eyes and swears under his breath.

"Jesus. This is hard," he says.

A lump forms in my throat. "I know."

I'm sure he's going to walk away now. But, instead,
he leans closer. His nose brushes against my forehead,
and his breath tickles my ear. I sink into him. His chest

is warm and hard. I feel his heart pound beneath his thin T-shirt. Music echoes from the subway station, and neon glow lights flicker in the distance. Otherwise the tunnel is quiet, empty. None of the other partiers have ventured this far from the dancing.

I tilt my face toward Sam and try to study his expression in the darkness. This is the closest we've been in months, and it still feels like he's a million miles away. I want to press my body closer to his, I want to run my fingers down the line of his back, but I'm not sure what's allowed. How close can I get before he pulls away again?

"Sam," I whisper. He stiffens. Want beats at my chest like a living thing, but I lose my nerve. I shift my body away from his, trying to ignore the fire spreading through my cheeks. "We were going to go back to the party. Remember?"

I curse myself as soon as the words leave my mouth. Sam frowns.

"Is that what you want?" he asks.

"What do *you* want?"

"I've been asking myself that question all night." He pushes a strand of hair behind my ear. I move closer.

"And did you come up with an answer?"

Sam lowers his face to mine without another word and kisses me. His stubble tickles my cheek. The world around me fades, and I'm only aware of him, and us, and being here together. I weave my arms around his shoulders, pulling him close. My fingers slide through his hair.

Sam pulls away, just for a second, and icy air finds all the spaces where his hands once were. "Maybe we should go slower this time," he whispers. "Not rush into anything."

I kiss him on the lips and the chin. "Yeah," I say, but before the word is out of my mouth, he's kissing me again.

Sam slips a hand under my shirt, pressing his fingers flat against my stomach. His thumb brushes the edge of my pants, and his pinkie slips beneath my bra.

Ever since we first started dating, I knew I wanted Sam to be my first. But something always stopped us.

He moves his hand around my waist, to my back. He slides his hand farther up under my shirt and grazes the back of my bra. I don't know how it happens, exactly, but suddenly I'm pressed against the cold brick wall, and then we're on the ground and Sam's on top of me.

The tunnel floor feels rough against my back. Cold seeps up through the concrete and chills the skin beneath my thin tee. I try to shift my weight to the side, and my elbow brushes against the metal train rail. This isn't how I imagined it would happen.

But then Sam moves from my mouth to my neck, leaving tiny kisses along my shoulders. I can't remember why we were waiting anymore. We love each other.

A single candle flickers from a few yards away, and a slow song starts over the speakers. I can't hear the words, but the beat vibrates through the ground. Sam moves his hand to my jeans, hesitating near the zipper.

"It's okay," I whisper. I reach for the edge of his T-shirt and push it up, revealing his flat, muscular stomach. Sam flushes and pushes his shirt back down.

"No, it's not." He moves off of me and sits. "We should talk."

I sit up and pull my top back down. Sam's jaw clenches. He stares at the train tracks instead of looking me in the eye.

"What's the matter?" I ask. Sam still doesn't look at me.

"Listen," he says. "I've been a wreck the last few months."

"Sam—"

"No, you should hear this," he interrupts. "I never wanted to break up with you. But I thought that if I left, you might turn things around."

"I understand." I brush my hand across my face. "And I did. The trust thing is going to be hard. I get that. But I'm done lying to you."

"No." Sam finally looks up at me. In the dim light, his dark eyes look black. "This isn't about you, Casey. You were hurting and you needed help. I get that."

"I'm better now," I insist. He squeezes my hand.

"I know. But I was hurting, too. I did some things. Made mistakes."

All at once I understand what he's trying to say. I drop his hand, feeling suddenly cold. "You were with someone else."

He stares at me, eyes pleading. "Just once. It didn't mean anything."

Who was it? The question beats at my temples, but I can't ask it. I think of all the gorgeous girls crowding around the stage during Sam's concerts. I picture one of them touching him, kissing him, and anger flares inside me. Not knowing is bad, but knowing would be worse.

"It doesn't matter," I say, and I try to believe it's true. I kiss Sam, but he doesn't kiss me back.

"Casey," he says. I shake my head.

"No. All that's behind us now." I kiss him again, harder, trying to bridge the space between us. "We were broken up. It doesn't matter."

Sam presses his mouth to mine, and his tongue slips past my lips. I melt into him, trying not to think about who he was with or our breakup or anything else. I pull him close. He's *Sam.* I tangle my hands in his hair and wrap my arms around his shoulders. All that matters is that we're together again.

Someone clears her throat. I pull away, looking up. Shana is standing over us, one eyebrow cocked.

"Sorry to break up the hot makeout sesh." She drains what's left in the red Solo cup she's holding and tosses it to the ground. Sam pulls himself off me, his cheeks flaming.

"Hey, Shana," he mutters, adjusting his shirt.

"Hiya, Sammy," Shana says. I frown. *Sammy?*

117

I stand and stumble over my feet. I reach for the wall to steady myself.

"Wow," Shana says, snickering. "Still enjoying that little treat I gave you earlier?"

"Treat?" I round on Shana. "You're unbelievable."

"Casey." Sam stands and grabs me by the shoulders. I yank my arm away. I've never hit anyone before, but I have the sudden urge to slap Shana across the face.

Confusion flickers through Shana's eyes. "What's your deal?" she asks.

"What's my *deal*?" I echo. "You drugged me!"

Shana's mouth curls into a smile. "You're welcome."

"What is the matter with you?" I say. I'd always known Shana was impulsive and a little selfish, but I had never seen her be cruel before.

"God, take a pill," Shana mutters. "You used to be *fun*."

"*Fun*?" I grit my teeth together. "That's your idea of fun?"

Shana moves closer, forcing me to take a step backward. "Precious," she says in a too-sweet voice. "We're at a *party*. I was helping you relax."

Relax. That word jogs something loose in my memory. Something I'd tried to forget. A night out with Shana was always epic. That didn't mean it was always fun.

For a while last year, she dated this guy named Jasper. He was probably in his twenties, but he looked older. He had a face like a catcher's mitt, all cracked leather and deep lines. Shana liked him because he had a motorcycle and a tattoo of a naked mermaid on his bicep. I never liked him. His eyes lingered for too long, and he had a way of touching you when he didn't need to.

Shana dragged me to a party at his house once. She said it was a barbecue. I figured we'd hang out in someone's backyard, eating hot dogs and drinking beer.

But Jasper's house didn't have a backyard. It didn't even have a front door. Shana and I pushed past an old, stained sheet and made our way into a dark living room without any furniture. A couple of guys sat on a bare mattress, smoking pot and drinking whiskey right out of the bottle. A strung-out girl with greasy hair snorted a line of coke off a piece of cardboard.

"Relax," Shana said. "It's a party. Have fun."

She kissed me on the cheek, and then she and Jasper disappeared into a back room. Leaving me alone.

I close my eyes, forcing the memory away. After that night, I swore I'd never go out with Shana again. But she called the very next weekend, talking about some insane concert that we couldn't miss. Before I knew it, I was texting her pics of outfit possibilities and asking her when she'd pick me up.

Sam's words echo through my head. *You acted different whenever you hung out with her. It's like the girl I loved was gone.*

This is what he was talking about. The second I got

around Shana I became the kind of girl who allowed herself to be drugged by someone she thought was a friend. I was stupid and desperate. A sidekick.

"I'm done," I say. Shana lifts an eyebrow.

"With what?"

"You." I cross my arms over my chest, willing myself to be strong. "I thought this kind of stuff just happened, but it's you. You're like a bad luck charm. I'm sick of it."

"*I'm* the bad luck charm?" Shana shakes her head, her lips twisted into a humorless grin. "Who *were* you before I came along? Suburban soccer Barbie?"

I push past Shana before she can say another word. She stumbles back, almost tripping over a train track.

"Watch it," she snaps.

"Or what?" I rake my hand through my hair. "What can you possibly do to me?"

I start down the dark tunnel, back toward the party. I've only gone a few feet when I step on something small and round. It shoots out from under my shoe and rolls across the ground, pinging against the nearest train track.

I'm not sure why, but I hesitate. A prickle of familiarity crawls up my neck. I pull my phone out of my pocket and aim it into the darkness.

Julie's black onyx ring glimmers from the ground, reflecting the light back at me.

"What's that?" Sam walks up behind me as I bend over to pick up the ring. Cold creeps into my legs and seeps through my body. If Julie's ring is here, then Julie was here.

"This is Julie's," I say, holding the ring up for Sam to see. He takes it from my hands.

"You think she lost it?" he asks.

"No," I say. Julie never takes this ring off. It belonged to her grandmother. If she lost it, she'd be on her hands and knees in this tunnel right now.

Unless something happened to her.

"Casey, no." Sam sees the look of horror cross my face and shakes his head. "That's not what this means."

"I saw her," I say, my voice trembling.

"You were high. It was a hallucination!"

I snatch the ring back from Sam's hands. "*This* is real!" I say.

Shana comes up behind Sam. "Done with your tantrum?" she asks me.

"When was the last time you saw Julie?" I ask.

Shana shrugs. "I don't know. A couple hours ago?"

A few hours. The image of her lying on the floor of the tunnel flashes through my mind. I see the dried blood on her tank top, the gaping wound in her chest. My knees wobble beneath me.

"We have to find her," I say. "Now."

TWELVE

"JULIE ALERT!" SHANA SHOUTS OVER THE MUSIC.
"That's her, right?"

She points to a girl in all black dancing near the edge
of the subway platform. The girl's thin, like Julie, and she's
wound her dark curls into a bun on top of her head. Hope
sparks inside me, and I start pushing through the crowd
to get to her. The strobe lights flash on and off, and I catch
a glimpse of her face. Not Julie.

"Let's try over there." I nod at the dwindling keg line.
We already searched the abandoned subway cars Woody
and Sam had performed in, and the paint-covered platform where Sam and I had played Twister. We're running
out of places to look.

Someone shuffles past me, spilling warm beer onto my
foot.

"Watch it!" I call over my shoulder. I start to turn back around, but a flash of sparkly tulle catches my eye.

Aya leans against the far wall, just below the blue tile sign that reads SOUTH FERRY. Her blue leopard-print dress glitters beneath the strobe lights. Woody's got his arm propped above her. His cow costume's gone, and he's buttoned a pink-and-orange Hawaiian shirt over his white undershirt and tight-fitting black jeans.

". . . I always thought I was a Capricorn," Woody's saying when we walk up to them. "And then I read some horoscopes for Aquarius . . ."

Aya glances at me and rolls her eyes.

"Where'd you get the shirt?" Shana asks

"Lost and found." Woody pops the collar. "You like?"

"Hey," I interrupt. "Has either of you seen Julie?"

"Not since she left with that guy." Aya glances at Shana, frowning. "I thought you went after her?"

"What guy?" I ask.

"That homeless guy," Aya says. "The one who led us down here. Julie wanted to take off, and he told her he knew where to find another exit."

"So she left?" Sam asks. I shake my head.

"No, I saw Lawrence less than an hour ago. He's still here."

"*Nice,*" Woody says. In a singsong voice, he adds, "Julie's getting some strange."

"Shut up, Woody," I say. I can still picture Lawrence's

unfocused eyes and the way his dreadlocks hissed at me like snakes.

Hallucinations, I think to myself. I close my eyes and rub my temples, willing my brain to work better. The dreadlock snakes weren't real, but Lawrence *was* there. He walked right into me.

I squeeze my hand into a fist, and Julie's ring digs into my palm. I think of the message scrawled across the tunnel walls. YOU'RE NEXT. Lawrence might be harmless, but someone down here isn't.

Woody frowns at me. "What's the big deal? So Julie hooked up with someone."

"I don't think that's what happened," I say.

"What's going on?" Aya asks. Panic creeps into her voice. She looks from me to Shana, and back to me again. "Casey, *tell* me."

"It's nothing," I say, praying that's true. I squeeze Aya's arm. "Did you see where they went?"

"I think so," Aya says. "Follow me."

The five of us weave through the party, following Aya toward another side tunnel jutting away from the main station. Rusty pipes twist across the tunnel ceiling and disappear into the darkness. The light's dim here, with fewer candles to illuminate the damp space. A few guys mill around the mouth of the tunnel, smoking.

"Wouldn't go down there," a guy with a buzz cut and thick eyebrows shouts over to us.

"Why not?" I ask.

"It's gross." He takes a puff of his joint.

"Did you see anyone else go down here?" I ask. "A girl with curly black hair?"

Buzz Cut runs a hand over his head. "Sounds familiar."

"She would've been with a guy," Sam adds. "He had long dreadlocks?"

Buzz Cut shrugs.

"Thanks anyway," I say, stepping into the tunnel. Old candy wrappers and grocery bags carpet the ground. A car drives overhead and tiny bits of rock crumble from the ceiling. Metal rails cut down the tunnel and twist into the darkness.

"Julie!" I shout. My voice booms around me, sounding big and hollow. But no one answers. We make our way deeper into the tunnels. I pick at the skin on my palms and dig my teeth into my lower lip—anything to keep myself from seeing Julie's blood-splattered hair. Her curled, lifeless fingers. The gaping hole in her chest.

No. I shake my head, forcing the images away. Even if I did see Julie lying in that tunnel, I could have hallucinated the blood and the chest wound and the rat. Lawrence's hair didn't really turn into snakes. He didn't have a serrated claw jutting out of his back.

"Julie's fine," I whisper to myself. Sam slides his hand into mine.

"Of course she's fine," he says. "Remember the party in

the woods last year? We all thought Julie had drowned in the lake because no one had seen her, but she was in that cave with all the other stoners."

Sam raises my hand to his mouth and kisses the inside of my wrist. Some of the tension leaves my shoulders. I'd completely forgotten about that party. We'd been about to call the cops, but it turned out Julie had just had a little too much pot. She passed out in the cave and didn't hear us calling for her.

Another tunnel veers off the main one. Rat eyes glow back at us from the darkness. They skitter into the shadows as we walk past.

"Maybe we should go back," Aya says. "I don't think she's down here."

I glance back the way we came. The tunnel entrance has disappeared in the darkness. I can't even see the smokers anymore.

"It doesn't look like anyone comes down here," Shana agrees.

There's no graffiti on the walls, no food wrappers littering the floor. Even the smell is different, like earth instead of beer and urine.

Sam aims his cell light farther down the tunnel. The dim beam moves over brown walls and rusted train tracks.

"We can head back to the station and check the other tunnels, too." He glances back at me and gives me a comforting smile. "We'll find her."

We make our way back toward the party in silence. The faint sound of music echoes through the tunnel. I keep my eyes narrowed, waiting for the darkness to open up into a subway station again. Minutes tick past, but the entrance doesn't seem any closer. I clench and unclench my hands. We should be there by now.

The tunnel wall curves, becoming a black grate set against the bricks. Narrow metal slabs stretch from the ceiling to floor. Music floats through the gaps, and glow lights flash in the darkness. I stop walking.

"That wasn't here on the way down," I say, touching one of the grimy bars. Woody leans in to peer through the grate.

"Cool," he says. "You can see the party."

"Not cool." Chills creep up my neck. "We didn't pass this on the way down. We must've taken a wrong turn."

"We just went straight, right?" Shana says.

"No, we turned left at that first tunnel," Aya adds. "Remember? You put a beer can at the entrance to remind us which path we went down?"

"Shit," Shana mutters. "I forgot about that."

My heart starts beating faster. "So we're lost?"

"We're not lost." Sam blows air out through his teeth. "The party's right there; we just have to figure out how to get back."

I peer through the grate. A lane of train tracks stretches past us, followed by a row of concrete pillars. The party's just on the other side. If I squint, I can see the subway platform and the line to the keg.

I loop my fingers through the metal slats and pull, trying to rattle the grate. It holds fast.

"We can't get through this thing, but the entrance we came through is over there." I point back down the way we came. "We'll have to backtrack to—"

Angry voices echo through the grate, interrupting me.

"What the hell?" Shana mutters.

Someone cuts the music. Thick white beams of light pierce the darkness, and the people crowded on the platform scatter like bugs. I lean in closer, squinting past the metal.

"Break it up!" a deep voice shouts. Cops swarm the station. I can just make out the blue of their uniforms.

"Shit," Woody says. "We have to go."

He takes a few steps toward the direction we came from, but I grab his arm.

"Wait! We can't leave without Julie," I say.

"Case, give it up. Julie's not here," Woody says. "She found an exit and left, end of story. Maybe she hooked up with someone else?"

I tell Woody about the bouncer standing guard near the tunnel entrance. "No one leaves Survive the Night till the party's over."

"Well, the party's over now." Woody slides his arm around my shoulder and guides me down the tunnel. "Besides, Julie's smart. If she wanted to get out of here, she could have found a way. If Lawrence didn't help her find an exit, she probably slipped the bouncer a few bucks."

The yelling on the other side of the grate fades as we hurry back down the tunnel. Woody finds the beer can Shana left to mark our path.

"This way," he calls, pointing us back to the main entrance. The others shuffle after him, but I hesitate. Another tunnel stretches to our left. I stare into the darkness and the skin along the back of my neck prickles.

"Casey, come on," Sam says. "Woody's right. She probably doubled back."

"But what if she didn't?" I step into the tunnel, fumbling for the light on my phone. "What if—"

A moan drifts from the darkness, cutting me off. I freeze.

"What was that?" Aya whispers.

Sam touches my arm. He stares down the tunnel, his eyes wide. "That didn't sound like Julie," he says.

Something moves. It sounds like nails on concrete. My phone suddenly feels heavy in my hand. All I have to do is switch on the light and shine it into the darkness. But I can't move.

"Shit," Shana hisses. "Casey, let's *go*."

"No." I turn my phone on, my fingers slick with sweat. The beam illuminates the toe of my leather ballet flat. I stare down at the circle of light, trying to steady my breathing.

My hands tremble as I lift the phone and cast the light into the shadows.

Julie's body stretches across the tunnel, her arms tied to the pipes twisting across the ceiling. Her hands are white as death, save for the purple bruises blossoming around her wrists. Her fingers curl toward her palms, and even from here I can see the black line of dried blood crusted beneath her nails.

Horror wraps around my chest like a vise. I drop to my knees.

"Oh my God," I say. The phone slips from my fingers and clatters to the ground. But the light stays on, illuminating Julie's body from below.

Intestines spill from the gruesome hole in the center of her stomach, glistening. Her head lolls forward and tangled hair hangs over her face. Blood drips from the curls and hits the concrete.

THIRTEEN

THE ROPES BINDING HER TO THE PIPES CREAK. HER body lurches forward, dripping fresh blood onto the dirt floor. I stifle a scream, terrified the ropes will unravel and send her crashing down on top of me.

But the ropes hold. Her body sways back into place.

Aya sinks to the ground, screaming. I should help her, but I'm frozen. I stare at Julie's curled fingers. Someone peeled the fingernail off her pinkie, leaving behind only raw, bloody skin. I wonder if she was alive when that happened. I wonder if she screamed.

"Holy shit!" Shana grabs my arm, her fingernails digging into my skin. Woody crouches at the side of the tunnel, vomiting. I feel a brush against my arm and jerk back.

"Casey." Sam holds both hands in front of him, his

voice steady. I get the feeling he's said my name a couple of times already. "We have to go."

Go? I look back at Julie, careful to keep my eyes focused on her neck and hair so I don't see the wound. "We can't leave her," I say. I picture the rats creeping from the shadows, climbing the walls. Another sob rises in my throat. Sam tries to touch my arm, but I pull away.

"We have to get her down!" I'm dimly aware of the hysteria in my voice. Julie's only a few feet off the ground, but I can't reach the ropes tied around her wrists, or the pipes jutting across the ceiling. I stand on my tiptoes. "Help me!"

"She's dead." Aya hiccups, and lowers her face to her hands. "Oh my God. She's *dead*."

Shana pulls her hands through her hair. "Damn it!" she yells. Her voice cracks, and she kicks the side of the tunnel. A trail of concrete crumbles from the wall.

Sam grabs my shoulders and spins me around. I try to pull away, but he holds tight.

"Let me go!" I pound at his chest with my fists. "We have to *help* her!"

"Listen to me," Sam says. Fear rings his eyes, making them wide. Manic. He clears his throat, struggling to keep his voice steady. "Whoever killed Julie is still down here. We have to go. Now."

His words shut everyone up. Aya chokes back a sob and stumbles to her feet. Shana wraps her arms around her chest.

There's movement in the darkness beyond Julie's body. I don't see it, but I feel the air shift around me and I hear something large and heavy drag across the ground. The reality of our situation hits me like a punch to the gut. Julie isn't just dead. She's been murdered. Someone murdered her.

My eyes travel to the wound in her stomach. Raw meat stares out from the gaping hole. The flesh looks shredded, like it's been put through a lawn mower. Blood clumps around her ruined skin, and intestines drip from her gut in a gruesome, glistening tangle. I can see the moldy walls through the wound. Something tunneled straight through Julie's body.

Julie's body rocks forward again and a bloody eyeball hits the ground with a sickening plop. It rolls across the tunnel, stopping at the toe of my shoe. The familiar brown iris stares up at me.

I scream, and fear makes my knees buckle. Sam grabs my arm and drags me back to my feet. He says something, his voice urgent.

Then we're running. Our shoes slap against the damp, trash-strewn ground and our breathing comes in gasps. My heart pounds in my ears, like a drum. We're so loud.

Everyone in the tunnels must hear us. I glance behind me, but the darkness is perfect. It presses against our backs like a solid thing.

We run forever. My legs ache and my lungs burn, but whenever I think of slowing, I remember the sound of Julie's eyeball hitting the ground and push myself to move faster.

A familiar sound echoes through the darkness behind us, raising the hair on the back of my neck. It's so quiet I'm not sure it's real.

Footsteps. Slow, steady ones.

My heart quickens, and I push myself faster, *faster*, ignoring the dull pain spreading through my bad knee. I think of how long it took us to get down here. It felt like we spent hours wandering around in the dark, calling Julie's name. The phantom footsteps seem louder now. Closer.

The tunnel opens into a wide space. The subway station. It looks bigger now that everyone's gone. Crushed Solo cups and beer cans litter the platform, and half the candles have blown out. The few still lit send ghostly shapes over the walls and fill the space with eerie light.

Sam and Woody dash past the platform, but Aya doubles over next to the wall, trying to catch her breath. Her sobs grow louder.

"Oh, God," she moans. "Oh, *God*."

"Quiet!" I grab her trembling arm and listen for footsteps. I don't hear anything, but I can't shake the feeling that someone's waiting in the dark. Watching.

Shana skids to a stop next to us. "We have to run," she hisses.

"I can't," Aya says, sniffling. Shana grabs her by the shoulders.

"If you don't move, you're going to die," she says. She pushes past Aya and runs after the boys without looking back. Nerves crawl over my skin, but I shake them away and hurry after her. I tug on Aya's arm and she stumbles behind me, still sobbing.

"Hurry!" Woody shouts, racing toward the tunnel at the far side of the cavernous space. We tear past the tracks and down the tunnel, to the ladder that leads back up to the surface. A single lit candle remains, casting light over the bottom rungs. Aya reaches the ladder first, but her hands shake so badly she can't hold on to the rungs. She pulls herself off the ground, then freezes.

I step up behind her and touch her hand. "What is it?" I ask. Silent tears roll down her cheeks, smearing her blue eyeliner.

"We're gonna die," she whispers.

"We're not going to die." I fight to keep my voice steady, and clench my hands into fists so Aya won't see how badly they're shaking. "We're getting out. You have to climb."

She shakes her head, tightening her grip on the ladder. Sam sucks in a breath.

"Even if you get her to climb, she won't be able to lift the manhole cover," he says. Woody moves to Aya's side and gently pries her fingers off the ladder.

"Let me go first?" he asks. Aya nods and he eases her back to the ground.

"We're going to die," she whispers again, but I think I'm the only one who hears her. I slip an arm around her shoulder and peer into the shadows. I keep expecting my vision to adjust, for the darkness to separate into a floor and walls and a ceiling. But if anything, it seems even darker than before.

Woody pulls himself onto the ladder, and the metal groans beneath his weight. A footstep thuds in the shadows. The sound is short and sudden and close. Woody freezes, and the rest of us turn to stare into the darkness. It occurs to me that we're all standing in a pool of candlelight that feels, suddenly, like a bull's-eye. I hold my breath, listening.

Silence.

Woody swears and starts climbing again. Faster.

"Hurry," Shana hisses. Her voice sounds more angry than scared, but her eyes cut to the shadows, and she can't stop tapping her foot.

One by one, my friends pull themselves up the ladder.

The metal screeches and moans beneath their weight. I listen but hear nothing outside our circle of candlelight. I wish this comforted me, but instead, I think of a lion crouching in the tall grass, watching his prey from a distance. Silence doesn't mean we're alone.

Aya climbs up next, and I pull Julie's ring from my pocket as I wait my turn. The shiny black onyx catches the candlelight.

I slip her ring onto my finger and twist it so the stone faces my palm. I curl my hand into a fist, letting the onyx dig into my skin. Sharp pain shoots through my hand, but I don't stop squeezing.

Julie was special. Anyone who talked to her could see that. She was in Honors English with me last year. She sat next to me the day our teacher, Ms. Lipton, covered an entire wall with plastic wrap.

"Every day I'll write a new word on the wall," Ms. Lipton explained. "If you use it in a paper you get one point of extra credit . . ."

Julie was slouched across the desk next to mine, her dark hair covering her face. A pencil dangled from her fingers. I thought she was asleep. But then she tapped the pencil against her desk. Tap. Tap. Pause. Tap.

Morse code. She taught me over the weekend, so we could talk, secretly, in class. I grinned, and scribbled the message in the corner of my notebook.

Ms. Lipton has lipstick on her teeth.

I don't realize I'm crying until I taste salt on my lips. I wipe my cheeks with the backs of my hands. Crying won't bring Julie back. Nothing will.

Something shuffles through the dark.

I'm suddenly alert. *A rat*, I think. But it sounded bigger.

Heart pounding, I pick the candle off the floor and step away from the ladder.

"Casey!" Sam hisses.

My candlelight illuminates only walls and floor and empty beer cans. I swing the candle away from my body, shedding the light as far as it will reach. There's nothing there.

Aya scurries up the ladder, leaving enough space for me to climb up behind her. I don't want to turn my back on the tunnels, but the other option is waiting down here alone. I carefully place the candle back on the ground. Aya climbs higher, and the space widens. I tighten my fingers on the rung and pull myself off the ground. I think I see something out of the corner of my eye, but I don't slow down long enough to look.

I catch up to Aya quickly. She's frozen again, staring up at the others. I hear pounding, and flinch. But it comes from above us, not below.

"What's wrong?" I shout. I can just make out the brown bottoms of Woody's Converse sneakers above Sam's head. He swears loudly, then bangs his fist against the manhole cover. The sound echoes through the tunnel.

"It's stuck," he shouts. "We're trapped."

Above me, Aya releases a horrified sob. "We're going to die."

FOURTEEN

"TRAPPED?" I WHISPER. I'M ONLY A FEW FEET OFF the ground, but I can't make myself pry my fingers off the ladder. Horror holds me in place. "Are you sure?"

The brown soles of Woody's sneakers shift on the rung above Sam. I stare at them, willing them to climb higher. Woody bangs against the manhole cover.

"Let us out!" he shouts. He pounds again, and the entire ladder shakes. I curl my fingers around the rungs and close my eyes. Shana swears and Aya releases another choked sob.

"Careful," Sam says.

I barely even notice the shaking. I'm too distracted by the darkness pressing in around us. I cling to the ladder, like a worm dangling on a hook. I make myself count to ten. Quickly, first. Then slowly.

One. Two. Three.

The last time I counted like this was the night Shana ditched me at Jasper's party. I stood frozen in the middle of that creepy living room, hands shaking as, one by one, everyone turned to stare at me. The men were worn out, like Jasper. They had watery eyes and cracked lips.

One of them leaned forward, and the bare mattress creaked beneath his weight.

"I heard about you." He bared his teeth. It wasn't quite a smile. "Shana brought you to keep me company."

He shook a whiskey bottle at me, like I was a dog he was trying to bribe.

"What are you talking about?" I asked him. Sweat plastered his hair to his head, and his jeans drooped low around his bony waist. He would have been cute, but drugs had hollowed out his cheeks and left his eyes vacant and cloudy.

"Just last week I asked Shana why she didn't share any of her friends with us." He licked his cracked lips. "She said she had a real hot piece for me. And here you are."

I cursed Shana in my head. "I have a boyfriend."

The man stood and stepped toward me. I could see his ribs through his thin T-shirt. "Sure you do," he said.

I raced for the bathroom without another word, pulling the door shut behind me. I crouched on the cold tile, trying to steady my breathing. I counted to ten over and over, and when that didn't calm me down, I dug a pill out of my pocket. Oxycodone, left over from my knee surgery. I bit into the pill, closing my eyes as it dissolved on my tongue. Then I pulled out my cell phone and dialed Sam's number with trembling fingers.

Woody bangs against the manhole cover, startling me back to the present. Sam says something, but his voice is too low for me to hear. I catch sight of a strand of Shana's pink hair and look away, angry. I don't know why I'm surprised when shit like this happens anymore. Shana ruins everything she touches.

There's a shuffle above us. Sam climbs up next to Woody, and both of them pound against the cover together. Hope rises in my chest, and I grip the ladder even tighter. But they stop pounding after a second. Sam swears.

"Climb down," he says.

No. I picture peeling my fingers away from the rungs, but it's like they've been glued into place. Julie was murdered down there. We can't go back.

"Casey," Sam whispers. "You have to go down."

I move my feet first, careful not to look into the shadows behind me. But the darkness seems to pulse. I picture it edging closer, the circle of candlelight growing smaller around us.

"Oh my God," Aya says when she drops to the ground next to me. She curls over herself, her shoulders shaking. "Oh my God, oh my God . . ."

"Shh . . . calm down." I slide my arm around Aya's

back, but she doesn't look at me. It's easier to feel strong when I'm comforting her. She starts to rock, and for just a moment, I forget my own fear.

"Oh my God," she whispers. "We're gonna die, we're gonna die."

She says this over and over again, until the words lose meaning. Or maybe I don't want to think about what they mean. Her voice carries through the silent tunnel. It bounces off walls and travels far into the darkness. Fear creeps back into my bones as I push the sweaty hair off Aya's forehead and try to quiet her. Her sobs will call Julie's murderer right to us. Unless the murderer knows where we are already.

"We're gonna die," Aya repeats in a shaky, desperate voice. Shana crawls down from the ladder.

"Can't you shut her up?" she asks. She leaps to the ground, her boots silent on the concrete. I don't want her help, but she huddles next to me, anyway.

"She's scared," I say. Shana raises an eyebrow, giving me a look halfway between "duh" and "what the hell are you talking about?"

"Or don't you remember that we found one of our best friends *dead* a few minutes ago," I snap.

"I remember," Shana says, her voice pure venom. She steps past me and takes Aya's chin, tilting her head so the candlelight illuminates her face. Aya's eyes are rimmed in red, her pupils dilated. "She's high."

"Aya doesn't get high," I point out, even though I saw her stoned off her mind just a few hours earlier. Aya usually avoids drugs and cigarettes, claiming they're bad for her skin. And whatever she's on now is a lot stronger than pot. "Did you drug her, too?"

Shana doesn't look at me. She bends down, and her pink-tipped hair sweeps over her forehead. She looks like she's going to kiss Aya on the cheek or whisper something in her ear.

Instead, she slaps her across the face. The sharp sound of skin hitting skin echoes around us.

"Hey!" Fury rears inside me. I grab Shana's shoulders and shove her back, angling myself between her and Aya. Aya releases another hysterical sob. "What the *hell* is wrong with you?" I hiss.

Shana pushes her hair behind her ears. "I thought it would help."

I glare at her as Aya crumples against my shoulder, sobbing and rocking.

"I'm pretty sure you made her worse," I say, patting Aya's hair. Shana shakes her head and stares up at Woody and Sam.

"How could any of this be worse?" she mutters.

A drop of water hits the ground, sending every nerve in my body on edge. I whip around and stare. *It's nothing it's nothing it's nothing*, I repeat, like a prayer. Shana flinches and grabs my arm, her icy fingers circling my wrist. We wait like that, frozen. But nothing happens.

Woody climbs back down the ladder next, breaking the spell.

"That manhole cover isn't budging," he says, wiping his grimy hands on his jeans. "We should find another exit."

A short, nervous laugh bubbles from my lips. "You mean go *back*?"

"It'll be okay." Sam kisses me on the forehead and warmth flickers through my skin. "We'll stick together."

"You're kidding, right?" I scoot closer, and Sam wraps his arm around my shoulder. It makes me feel safer, if only for a moment.

"We don't really have a choice." Sam squeezes my arm. "The manhole cover is stuck."

Water drips from the tunnel's ceiling and hits my elbow. I flinch and huddle closer to the candle.

"We can't go back there." I glance up at Sam, wanting him to take my side. He stiffens.

"Casey—" he starts, using his "you're being unreasonable" voice. I step away from him, suddenly annoyed.

"She's right," Shana says before I can defend myself. She tries to catch my eye but I avoid looking at her. She always does this when she pisses me off. For the next hour or two she'll agree with everything I say, just to soften me up.

But I don't want to be softened up this time. Shana's the reason we're down here. She's the reason Julie's dead. I squeeze my eyes shut to keep the tears from leaking

onto my cheeks. I meant what I said to her before. I'm
done being her friend. I'm done with all of this.

Shana clears her throat and looks down at the toe of
her boots. "Who knows if we'll find another exit?"

"That one is stuck!" Sam says. "We can't just stay here
and bang on it like a bunch of idiots!"

"We could spend more than two minutes trying to get
it open," I insist.

"Someone could walk by and hear us." Aya stands,
wobbling a little on her heels. Tears stream down her face,
but she brushes them away with her palm. "They might
stop to help."

"No one would help," Shana mutters. Even I can't bring
myself to agree with Aya. It's somewhere around four
o'clock in the morning in a shady neighborhood in Lower
Manhattan and we're pounding on a manhole cover.

"I tried everything," Woody says.

"Shit." Shana tries to look at me again, but when I don't
meet her eyes, she turns to Sam. "There are still some
candles left burning. If we go now, we might be able to
find another exit before they go out."

So much for being on my side. "I'm not going back
there," I say.

"Jesus! What is your problem?" Shana snaps, shoving
her hands in her pockets.

Sam drops a hand on my shoulder and squeezes. "Guys,
drop it," he says. "We have bigger issues right now."

Shana stares at his hand. Her eyes narrow.

"I get it." Her mouth twists into a cruel smile. "The lovebirds talked things over and decided this is my fault. Everything's my fault, isn't it?" She turns to Sam, narrowing her eyes. "You're acting like I forced you into something but I was *there*. You wanted it just as bad as I did."

You wanted it just as bad as I did? The words repeat in my head, like a math problem I can't figure out. I frown and cross my hands over my chest. "What are you talking about?"

Shana's eyes widen. She looks from me to Sam. "I thought you . . . shit."

"What do you mean *shit*?" Something nags at me, but I brush it away. I'm being paranoid. I turn to Sam, but he won't meet my eyes. "What's going on?" I ask. The nagging feeling gets stronger, more insistent.

"Nothing." Shana shakes her head. She stares down at her boots. The nagging feeling is different now. It's panicked and ugly—desperate. I turn back to Sam, heat rising in my face.

"You said you were with someone." My voice shakes, but I force the words out, anyway. "When we were broken up."

"Casey . . ." He reaches for me, but I slap his hand away. I feel dirty where I let him touch me.

"Shana?" I hiss. "You were with *Shana*?"

I wait for him to deny it. To tell me I'm crazy, that he

would never hook up with my best friend. But he can't even meet my eyes. Dread forms a lump in the pit of my stomach. I picture him looking at her, touching her skin, and my stomach turns. Sam's face looks ashen. Guilty. "I tried to tell you," he says.

"You were giving me shit for hanging out with her. And all along you . . ." I can't even say the words. I'm going to be sick.

"I know," Sam says. "That was wrong, I'm sorry."

I close my eyes. His words mean nothing to me. They're static. White noise.

"You were broken up," Shana adds, like this explains everything. I round on her. All the frustration and anger I've felt since she spiked my drink bubbles up inside me. I'm an idiot for thinking she actually cared about me. She doesn't care about anything or anyone but herself.

"Everyone said you were a bitch. I actually thought you were my friend," I say.

Shana stares at me for a beat. Then her lips curl into a smirk that's halfway between embarrassed and proud. "Don't be a tease. You like me because I'm a bitch. You wish you were more like me."

I have to curl my hand into a fist so I don't slap her.

"Shana, stop." Sam shoots her a look.

"Shut up, Sam," I hiss. I don't want his help. I don't want anything from him.

"Oh, calm down, Case." Shana frowns. "It didn't mean anything! We were just having fun."

"Of course you were!" I shout. "You're always having fun. Fun's the only thing that matters to you."

Sam takes a step toward me. "Casey, please," he says. "As soon as we get out of here, we'll talk. I can explain everything."

My whole body shakes with anger, but my voice is steady. Cold, even. I turn on Sam. "I *trusted* you."

Sam hunches his shoulders and stares at his feet. I see his lips on her neck. His hand slipping beneath her shirt. Disgust rises in my throat.

I have to get out of here.

I push past Sam and climb back onto the ladder. Anger propels me forward, and I move up the rungs two at a time, until the manhole is directly above me. I loop one arm around the ladder to steady myself, and run my fingers along the cool metal. There has to be a latch or a groove—something that Sam and Woody missed. But the surface is smooth. Frustration bubbles up inside me. I grit my teeth and bang against the cover with all my strength.

A dull ache forms at the back of my head. I close my eyes, trying to calm the steady beat of pain.

I feel like I'm at the clinic again. I'm huddled in the corner of my room that first night, sweat drawing lines down my back. I can't stop shaking. Tremors of pain roll through my body. My stomach churns, even though I haven't eaten since this morning. My arms trembling, I crawl to the foot of my bed and fumble for my sneakers. The painkiller I snuck in clatters onto the cold tile floor.

The door to my room creaks open, and a nurse walks in. My heart pounds wildly. I grope for the pill, but it slips from my sweaty fingers.

"Where did you get this?" The nurse kneels and picks my last pill up off the floor.

"I need that," I say, grabbing at her hands. She shakes her head and leaves the room, shutting the door behind her.

"No!" I shout. I crawl over to the door and bang against the wood until my knuckles bruise.

My eyes flicker open again. I'm in the tunnel, not rehab, and my knuckles are raw from pounding at the manhole cover. But it hasn't budged.

The headache seeps into my skull. I imagine it like a wild creature, its long tentacles pressing against my brain and temples.

My body feels heavier as I climb back down the ladder and drop to the ground next to my friends. "It's stuck."

"You don't say," Woody mutters, cocking an eyebrow.

The rest of them look at me, waiting. I wipe the grease from the ladder rungs onto the back of my jeans.

I don't want to think about what happens next, but Shana's right. It's better to get it over with now. Before the candles die.

"Okay," I say.

"Casey . . ." Sam puts a hand on my arm. The same hand that touched Shana's skin and hair and lips. I pull away, disgusted.

"Don't," I warn him. I still can't look him in the face, so I stare at the toe of his sneaker. "Let's find another exit and get the hell out of here."

Sam nods and peels the candle off the floor. The flame sparks as he holds it out in front of him.

"Let's go," he says.

FIFTEEN

SAM LEADS US DOWN THE TUNNEL, HOLDING THE candle in front of him like a beacon. Shana's arm brushes against his as they walk, and I look away.

I always thought she hated Sam, or that she was jealous of how much time I spent with him. Now I know better.

I should have figured it out the night of Jasper's party. I was crouched in the bathroom, waiting to be rescued by Sam, when I heard Shana's gravel-on-sandpaper voice on the other side of the plywood door.

"Where's Casey?" she demanded, but she started toward the bathroom without waiting for an answer. Her high-heeled boots bit into the floorboards, making them shake.

I wanted to crawl into the dirty shower stall and hide. I wanted to back up against the door and hold it shut with my body. But that was stupid. Shana was my best friend.

Seconds later, she threw open the bathroom door. "What are you doing in here?"

I swallowed, feeling the last grains of oxy dissolve on my tongue. "Hiding from that creep you left me with."

"That *creep* is our hookup. He's going to score us some H."

Shana wiggled her eyebrows, but I just stared. *H*. As in *heroin*.

"Are you crazy?" I hissed.

"Duh," Shana whispered, giggling. "Come on."

She started to stand, but I grabbed her wrist, pulling her back to the floor. "Wait," I said. "What did you promise him?"

Shana's smile faded. "What?"

"What did you say you'd give him in exchange for the drugs?"

Shana chewed her lip. Her eyes traveled down my body. "You wouldn't have to do much," she said. "Just make out a little."

Disgust turned my stomach. "*No*," I said. Shana started to argue, but a car rumbled to a stop outside, cutting her off.

"That's Sam," I told her.

Shana rolled her eyes. "Of course you called Prince Charming to come and save you," she muttered.

I pushed past her and dashed for the front door, ignoring the whistles and hollers that followed me out.

I kick a beer can, watching it rattle down the subway tunnel. Sam had been furious. He broke up with me the very next morning. It hadn't occurred to me until now that all of it had been Shana's fault. If she hadn't dragged me to that party, Sam never would have seen me like that. He wouldn't have dumped me, I wouldn't have been sent to rehab, and he never would have ended up with Shana. Everything would have been fine.

Woody elbows me. "You want?" he asks, holding a silver flask engraved with a marijuana leaf. I shake my head.

"No thanks."

Woody shrugs and takes a drink. "Right," he says. "Shana mentioned you were doing the whole sober thing."

"Yeah," I say. "They look down on drinking in rehab."

Woody nods, like I just said something deeply profound. "I get that." He takes another swig from his flask. "So. Are you a Jesus freak now?"

"What?" I cough.

"My cousin went to rehab last year. When she came back she was, like, *really* into Jesus. She started saying all this stuff about how *He* was driving her car, and that *He* takes over when she can't handle her life." Woody fumbles with the flask's lid. "Apparently there was a lot she couldn't handle, because she prayed all the time, too. I mean, she prayed like it was her job. Come to think of it, I don't think she had a real job."

"I'm not into Jesus now," I say, cutting him off. "It wasn't that kind of rehab."

Woody nods, solemnly, like he's well acquainted with

the many types of rehab. "Do you think it's God?" he asks. He stretches his arms over his head and his shirtsleeve moves up, revealing the Japanese characters he had tattooed on his bicep sophomore year. He thinks they read "peace" but Aya told me they actually say *kimoi*, which translates to "creep."

"Do I think what's God?" I ask.

"Whatever happened to Julie. Maybe it's the Rapture and God is killing all nonbelievers."

I think about the bloody wound hollowing out her gut and the way someone strung her up across the tunnels for us to find. I twist Julie's ring around my thumb. It's too big for me, and I'm afraid it'll slip from my finger. "It's not the Rapture," I say.

"Then what do you think it is?

Something thuds to the ground ahead of us. I stop walking and grab Woody's arm.

"Oh, God," Aya moans. "Oh God oh God oh God." She huddles against Shana's back.

Sam squints into the darkness, holding the candle before him. The light illuminates only the rough stone-and-brick wall. "I think it was just some dirt crumbling from the ceiling," he says.

We start shuffling forward again. It definitely could have been dirt, I tell myself. These walls are old enough. I'm surprised we don't hear more bits and pieces crumbling off them.

But the noise didn't really sound like dirt.

I huddle closer to Woody, pushing that thought to the very back of my mind. He drops a hand on my shoulder and squeezes. It's a nice, brotherly gesture and I feel a rush of gratitude toward him.

"Well?" Woody asks. "What do you think it is?"

It's a second before I remember that he's asking me what I think killed Julie. "I think it was a man," I say. He raises an eyebrow, and I tell him about the girls I heard talking about the homeless serial killer who lives in these tunnels.

Woody blows air out through his teeth. "That's messed up," he mutters. "Do you think he's down here now?"

I stare straight ahead, into the darkness that's like a wall outside the safety of Sam's candlelight. If I think too hard about all the things that could be hiding out there, I wouldn't be able to take another step. I swallow, and the back of my throat tastes like ash.

"Yeah," I say. "I think he's down here now."

We continue moving through the tunnels in silence, eventually reaching a fork. Woody gives my shoulder one last squeeze and jogs up next to Sam.

"This way," he says, pointing down a narrow tunnel that twists away from the main subway system. It's much smaller than the tunnels we've been walking through so far, and there aren't any tracks stretching across the ground.

Sam frowns. "You're sure?" he asks.

"I practically *live* in the subways," Woody says. A clump of blond hair falls over his forehead, and he gives his head a practiced toss to get it out of his eyes. "This one's headed north, yeah? Should take us to Chambers. There's definitely a way out there. We'll probably find something after, like, twenty minutes of walking."

"*Twenty* minutes?" Shana hisses.

"Tops," Woody says.

"Look, if he thinks there's an exit this way, we should take it," Sam says. "Better than wandering around lost."

"I guess," Shana mutters.

The new tunnel is too narrow for us to walk side by side. We form a line—Woody, then Sam, Shana, Aya, and me. Our footsteps echo off the curved walls around us, and water drips from the ceiling. I slip my cell out of my jeans pocket and check the time—4:37 a.m.

We'll be out of here before five, I tell myself. I try to picture what will happen next. Would we go right to the police station to report Julie's murder? I imagine someone wrapping a blanket around my shoulders, and drinking watery coffee while I explain how we found her. The thought makes me shiver. It's equal parts comforting and horrifying.

The tunnel slopes upward. I lean forward to keep from losing my balance. A broken lightbulb juts out from the wall, and glass crunches beneath my feet. A cockroach darts over the bricks. I cringe, looking away.

The wall ends, abruptly, replaced by thick wooden slabs that stand several feet apart. Sam's candlelight flickers over another lane of thick metal rails on the other side.

I dig my cell phone out of my pocket and aim the light past the tracks. Chicken wire stretches between the two lanes. It comes up to my waist, affixed to the wood with bright orange zip ties. A wooden beam cuts across the slabs, dividing the space in half.

"Do you think there's something over there?" I crouch to peer below the beam, shining my light over another brick wall on the other side of the train tracks. "An exit or another platform?"

A train thunders through the tunnels before Woody can answer. I don't see it, but dirt rains down from the ceiling, coating my hair. My heart leaps in my chest. Trains mean people.

"There must be a working subway directly above us," Woody says, shaking the dust from his head.

"How do we find it?" Aya asks.

"The tunnel's sloping up," Woody says. "They should connect at some point."

The others hurry forward, but I stand too quickly and smack the back of my head against the wooden beam. Pain spreads through my skull and a wave of dizziness washes over me. For a second, I can't see.

"Shit," I mutter. Someone drops a hand on my shoulder. "It's okay," I say, rubbing my head. "I'm fine."

"Casey?" Woody calls. I blink, and my eyesight clears.

Sam and Shana huddle together at the far end of the tunnel, the candle flickering between them. Woody stands a few feet away, Aya hovering behind him.

They all stare at me, eyes wide with horror.

"Oh my God." Aya lifts a trembling hand to her mouth. Fear trickles through me.

I turn my head.

Meaty gray fingers rest on my shoulder. The flesh is mottled and waterlogged, the fingers swollen to twice their size. Jagged black nails jut out from them, looking like they might pop off. There's a raw, bloody wound where the pinkie should be.

I scream and jerk forward. The hand tumbles from my shoulder and smacks onto the dirt-covered floor. Two bones jut out of the bloody, decaying stump.

SIXTEEN

I STUMBLE INTO THE WALL, SWATTING MY ARMS and shaking out my hair. I still feel those fingers on my shoulder, the fingernails grazing my skin.

"Holy shit!" Woody shouts. Sam lunges forward and yanks me away from the decaying hand. I shudder violently. I can't seem to catch my breath.

Shana takes a step forward, her eyes wide. "What's that?" she says, and I jerk my head around to where she's staring.

The decaying remains of an arm stick out from a narrow crevice just above us. Bloody flannel rags cling to what's left of the jagged bones and shredded, meaty flesh. Nausea turns my stomach. I sink against the wall and ball up a fist at my mouth to keep from vomiting. I'm dimly aware of a cold hand brushing against my arm.

I flinch away.

"Hey, it's just me," Sam says, holding his hands in front of him. "Are you okay?"

"I'm okay." I take another deep breath and clench my hands to still the trembling. Sam aims the candlelight at the arm.

"It looks like he got caught on the tracks," Sam says, nodding at the arm. "See the rail? There must be another tunnel above us."

I squint into the shadows behind the arm. Metal train tracks glint back at me, barely visible through the crevice. I swallow. Maybe Sam's right. Maybe this poor man just got caught on the rails and lost his arm. I take a step closer, fear prickling the back of my neck. I can't help thinking of those girls I overheard at the party again.

They never found his body, they'd said.

"Let's go," I say. I swipe at my shoulder again, even though I know there's nothing there. "I want to get the hell out of here."

"Amen," Shana adds.

We hurry forward. I slide my phone back into my pocket. Then, thinking twice, I pull it back out and turn up the display. A narrow, bright spotlight appears in the inky darkness, illuminating the back of Aya's leopard-print dress. She flinches and glances over her shoulder at me.

Blue eyeliner streams down her cheeks, mixing with her tears. Her narrow black eyes look small without it.

Black hair falls loose from its fancy chignon and clings to her head, limp and lifeless.

"We're gonna die," Aya whispers, lips trembling. Her lipstick's gone, too, except for the faint smudges of red around the corners of her mouth. I lift my phone higher, but Aya flinches and shies away from the light before I can illuminate her pupils.

"Sorry." I reach for her hand. It feels skinny and fragile, like it belongs to a sick person, but then Aya squeezes my fingers, and she feels strong again.

"I'm so scared, Case," she whispers. She tries to keep a sob from escaping her lips, and her chest rises and falls. "We're gonna die. Just like Julie."

I picture gray skin and black fingernails. I feel the cold hand resting on my shoulder. My heart starts beating faster.

"We're not going to die." I squeeze Aya's hand. "Remember when we spent the night at Julie's house last summer?"

Julie's place is the only one with a finished basement, so we stayed over one weekend. Her mom set us up with popcorn and ordered pizza, and then left us alone for the rest of the night. We drank a bottle of peach-flavored champagne that Shana had stolen, and gossiped till four in the morning.

Aya stares past me, her small black eyes flitting about like a bird. I don't think she heard me. But she nods.

"She made us play that game," she says. "The scary one."

"The Ouija board," I say. Julie spent the whole night trying to freak us out. She made us say "Bloody Mary" into her bathroom mirror and kept trying to get us to tell scary stories. But the Ouija board was her favorite. She lit a bunch of candles and poured us all a glass of the sickly sweet champagne and announced that we were going to contact the spirit of some long-dead serial killer.

"Right," I say. "Remember how you couldn't sleep? And we stayed up half the night, painting each other's nails and talking, until you finally passed out on the couch. Remember?"

Aya nods. "I remember," she says.

I squeeze her hand. "And the next day, you woke up and realized there was nothing to be afraid of. That Julie just made everything up to scare us."

My phone blinks off. I hear Aya's raspy breathing in the darkness. I fumble for the power button and switch the phone back on again.

"But *this* is real," Aya says when the light hits her face. "And Julie's dead."

She pulls her hand away from mine and shuffles forward in silence. Every few minutes I hear her sniffle, and she wipes her cheek with her hand.

We follow Woody down one tunnel, and then another, deeper and deeper into the subway's depths. Sam's candle bobs ahead of me, and I play a game of letting it move farther and farther away. Like I don't care about him. But there's an empty space that grows larger as the distance between us stretches. I want to feel his arm around my shoulder, and I want to hear him say that everything's going to be all right, in his quiet, confident voice. He has the kind of voice you can't help believing.

I wrap my arms around my chest, trying to shake the feelings away.

I look away from the candlelight and check my phone— 5:12. I walk a little faster and open my mouth to call out to Woody. Something glimmers in the tunnel ahead. My mouth hangs open, but I forget what I was about to shout.

"What the hell was that?" Shana says.

"I think it was a light," Sam says. He starts moving faster. "Maybe this is Chambers."

We walk faster, hurrying toward the glimmer. The ground angles down slightly. The tunnel opens up and we spill into a wider, open space. A stone ceiling arcs high above us, and rounded brick walls surround us on all sides. Two more tunnels twist off from the walls, and all are just as narrow and dark as the one we came down. I look around the space for the glimmer—and step right into a puddle of water.

"What the hell," I mutter, shuffling back. Water seeps through my flimsy leather shoe and soaks the bottom of my jeans. Shana splashes into the puddle next to me.

"Shit," she says, staring down at her soaked leather

boot. Disappointment flashes across her face. "You guys, *this* must've been what we saw. Our lights reflected off the water."

We're quiet as it sinks in that we're no closer to finding an exit. I make my way around the side of the space, cringing as water seeps into my shoes. I use my phone to illuminate the two new tunnels. Water pools along the bottoms of both.

"This must be why these tunnels are closed," I say. Woody comes up behind me.

"Is that a sign?" he asks.

I frown. "Like, from God?"

He gives me a look and takes the phone out of my hand, sending a beam of light toward the wall. Faded black paint labels the tunnel.

CITY HALL, it reads. I glance at Woody, wondering if he recognizes the name. Frown lines crinkle his forehead.

"Shit," he mutters.

"What do you mean *shit*?" Sam asks.

Woody scratches the back of his head with my phone. "Look," he says. "I must've gotten a little turned around."

"Turned around?" Shana asks.

"I thought we were heading toward Chambers." Woody turns and glances at the sign reading CITY HALL. "But, um, it looks like we veered east at some point."

"We've been walking in the wrong direction for *half an hour*?" Sam yells.

His mouth is a hard, thin line. Heat climbs his neck, and red splotches color his cheeks. He rakes his hand through his hair and kicks the floor of the tunnel. Something skitters through the dark and splashes into the puddle.

"Damn it!" Sam shouts. Woody clears his throat.

"Look," he says. "I think . . ."

"I don't care what you *think*." Sam rounds on Woody and shoves him. Woody stumbles into the water and falls against the wall.

"Watch it!" he shouts. Sam stares daggers at him. For a second I'm sure he's going to hit him again, but then he shakes his head. Some of the anger fades from his face, and he offers Woody his hand.

"Sorry," he mutters, pulling Woody back to his feet. Woody shrugs and straightens his shirt.

"If you two are done, will one of you explain how we're going to get out of here now?" Shana asks.

Sam sighs, and looks over Shana's shoulder, down the tunnel we just walked through. "I guess we double back? See if we can find the way to Chambers?"

"Double back?" Woody shakes his head. "Look, there's definitely an exit down toward City Hall. A bunch of other trains crisscross the tunnels up there. It's probably just ten more minutes on."

"Um, it's flooded." Shana stomps around in the water with her heavy boots, splashing the walls. I resist the urge to roll my eyes. There's maybe an inch of water sloshing around on the ground and our feet are already wet.

"I'm up for going to City Hall," I say. "The water's not deep."

"Not *yet*." Shana cocks an eyebrow, looking at me like I'm crazy. "And the tunnel slopes down. We're trying to go up, remember?"

"So you want to turn around?" The idea of going back the way we came makes me feel suddenly very tired. "Come on, he said it was just ten more minutes!"

"He also said we were headed toward Chambers!" Shana shouts. "He doesn't know what he's talking about!"

"Hey, I don't see you helping," Woody says.

"Guys, stop." Sam moves between us. Turning to me, he says, "Look, we have to turn back."

Anger flares inside me. "Of course you'd side with Shana."

"I'm not siding with Shana. I'm trying to be logical about this." Sam slams his fist against the tunnel wall. "Woody doesn't really know where we're going."

"*Jesus*. That sign clearly says *City Hall*." Woody waves his hands at the faded black letters. "You do *see* it, don't you? I'm not hallucinating?"

"Well, what if we go down that tunnel and can't get back out?" Sam asks. "Or what if it's so badly flooded that we wind up trapped?"

"What if we head back the way we came and get *lost?*"
I shout back.

Something shuffles behind us, and I flinch before realizing it's just Aya. She steps away from the wall and puts her hand on my arm. Shana looks from me to her.

"I guess she's the tiebreaker," she mutters, crossing her arms over her chest. "Well, Aya? What do you want to do?"

Aya sniffs and rocks back and forth on her dirty heels. "I'm with Casey," she says, her voice raw from crying. "Let's go to City Hall."

SEVENTEEN

"WELL. THIS IS FUN," SHANA SAYS. *"GREAT* PLAN, guys."

She sloshes through the water, sending choppy waves crashing against the tunnel walls. We've only been walking for fifteen minutes, and the freezing water is up to our knees. My toes are numb.

Aya sniffles. "Ew. *Ew*," she whispers under her breath.

We made her take off her ridiculous heels back when the water started getting higher, and now she walks barefoot through the flooded tunnels. Algae climbs the walls and blankets the ceiling, and dusty pipes twist along beside us. Aya slips on something and stumbles forward, grabbing my arm. I pause to let her steady herself.

"You okay?" I ask. She sniffles.

"We're gonna die, Casey. We're gonna *die*."

She starts sobbing again. I turn my back instead of trying to help, and wade forward. Guilt clenches my stomach, but I try to ignore it. I know she's high and terrified, but I've tried talking to her and I've tried calming her down. Nothing works. The only thing we can do is get out of here as soon as possible.

"Seriously," Shana says. She swings her leg, kicking up a wave of greasy water. "It was too easy when we were just trapped underground with a serial killer. Now we get to be trapped underground *in a flooded tunnel* with a serial killer."

Aya whimpers, but Shana doesn't seem to notice.

"I've always wondered whether crocodiles lived in the subways," she says. "I guess now I'll find out. Thank you, Woody." Shana slow-claps, walking through the water backward.

"Don't be a bitch, Shana," Woody mutters.

Shana forms an *O* with her mouth and puts her hand to her chest in a mock "Who, me?" gesture.

A headache pounds at my temples. Aya inhales, and I hear that telltale hitch in her breathing that usually comes before she starts sobbing again. I know Shana's just letting off steam and that she's probably as freaked as the rest of us. But she doesn't seem to care that she's making everyone miserable.

"Let's talk about great plans, Shana," I say. "Like how it was such a great plan to bring us to this party. And losing track of Julie. That was a *fantastic* plan."

Shana releases a short laugh. "No one put a gun to your head, soccer Barbie. You could've gone home any time you wanted."

"You're joking, right? Or did you forget the giant, scary bouncer guarding the door? Oh, yeah, and that thing where you *drugged me?*"

"Like you weren't asking for it!"

"Shana, shut up," Sam says, cutting her off.

Shana stops walking, and hurt flashes across her face. She looks at Sam, then back at me. I can't help the little half smile that curves my lips.

We continue wading through the tunnel in silence. My cell phone light dances over grimy gray walls. I glance at the display.

"Ten percent," I shout. Sam's phone died a few minutes ago. Woody and I are the only ones who still have power left. We're trying to preserve it.

"You should turn it off until the candle goes out," Sam calls back to me. The candle burns low in his hand. There's not much wick left, and the flame is barely more than a dim, glowing ember. I switch my phone off and slip it into my back pocket.

Shana swears under her breath. "Now it's cold, wet, *and* dark," she mutters.

I glare at her back, twisting Julie's ring on my finger. I picture Julie sitting in the backseat of Shana's Buick, pinching her fingers together like she was meditating.

With her dark eyes and those thick curls falling down her back, she looked like a goddess. Before she got into pot, Julie was brilliant. Harvard brilliant. NASA brilliant. She had the best PSAT scores in our entire school.

I twist the ring around my finger. The metal cuts into my skin, leaving it raw. I barely notice. I'm thinking about the time Julie and I tried to study SAT vocab in the cafeteria during lunch. My parents had just bought me a bunch of expensive prep materials: new books and flash cards and practice tests. I showed them to Julie, but she sighed, shaking her head.

"These things have no soul," she told me. "You need to *be* the SAT vocabulary words to understand them."

We were still laughing when Shana bounced up to our table.

"Come with me," she said, smiling her little-kid smile. "I have a surprise."

We followed her to the edge of the parking lot, where Sid Bronson parked his van. Sid wasn't a student, but he hung around the school, selling fake IDs and drugs. Rumor was he didn't accept money. You had to pay him in favors.

My stomach twisted in knots as we stepped up to his van. Shana stood on her tiptoes and rapped on the rusty metal door. He unrolled the window a crack, and Shana slipped him a folded piece of notebook paper. To this day I have no idea what it said. A second later, Sid opened the door and handed her a tiny white envelope.

"It's X," she whispered as we walked away. "Just enough for the three of us."

Shame and fear gnaw at my insides when I think of that memory. Julie and I didn't even think. We just followed Shana blindly.

A tear oozes out of the corner of my eye. I wipe it away with the back of my hand. My head pounds, throbbing with regret.

I imagine Julie walking next to me. I wish I could grab her hand or hear her wry, sarcastic voice again. I close my eyes, whispering a silent prayer. *If I get out of this place, I'll take the SATs and apply to college. I'll go to sleepovers at Madison's house. I'll be a different person.*

I pull the Tylenol bottle out of my pocket. There are still a few pills rattling around inside. *I'll never touch anything stronger than Tylenol again*, I think to myself, popping off the lid. I look inside the bottle and freeze.

Two tiny, round oxycodone pills sit nestled among the remaining Tylenol. They stare up at me, beckoning.

All the air leaves my lungs. *Those pills can't be here.* I blink, but they're still there when I open my eyes. Waiting.

I slam the lid back on the bottle and shove it into my pocket. My parents said they swept my room and threw out all my old stashes. They could have missed a bottle.

Shana had your pills, a little voice in the back of my head says. I run a hand over the buzzed side of my head, thinking of how she had swiped the Tylenol bottle off the bar and handed it back to me later. It would've been just like her to give me a few pills. Like a dare.

Aya's breath hitches again. The sound is sharp, like a paper bag crumpling. I glance back at her, grateful for the distraction.

"How you doing, Aya?" I ask. Her skin looks pale beneath her streaked makeup. She hiccups.

"Oh God, oh God, oh God." She can't focus on my face. Instead, she stares at something over my shoulder. Nerves prickle along my neck. Something flickers at the corner of my eye. I whip around. But there's nothing there.

"Aya, I need you to calm down," I say. The oxy pills burn inside my pocket, but I ignore them. Aya's red-rimmed eyes slide over to mine and widen. She screams.

"Aya!" I say. She doesn't hear me. Her scream echoes through the tunnels. She sinks to her knees and her blue skirt floats to the surface of the water.

The others stop walking and crowd around me.

"Is she okay?" Woody asks. Aya wraps her arms around her chest. She stops screaming for long enough to suck down a lungful of air. Then her scream cuts through the tunnels again, shrill and piercing.

"I don't know." I frown, and touch her shoulder. Aya jerks away. Her eyes bulge, and her face turns red. "She was fine before. Well, not *fine*, but she wasn't freaking out."

"I'm starting to lose my cool," Shana says. I can hear the fear in her voice, and that scares me more than Aya does. I think of the oxy again, then curse myself. I'm not going to take it. I *refuse* to take it.

Aya's scream cuts off, abruptly. She stares at that same spot over my shoulder and rocks back and forth on her knees, hugging herself. Water laps around her waist. I have that feeling again, that feeling that someone's watching me.

Steeling myself, I turn around. The tunnel wall stands directly behind me. There's enough light to see the curve of it, but the details are in shadow. "No." Aya moans. "No no no no."

Fear drops through me like a rock. "Do you see something?" I pull my phone out of my pocket, illuminating her face with the blue-tinted phone display. The light washes out her skin, making her look like a ghost.

"Oh, God," she whispers. "*Oh, God.*"

"She's panicking," Sam says. He reaches for my hand, and this time I don't pull away. "I don't think she can hear you."

"There's something there." I nod at the opposite wall. Sam wades through the water to stand beside me.

"I'm scared," I admit. He squeezes my fingers.

"On three," he says. "One. Two . . ."

He lifts his candle, and I raise my phone, illuminating the tunnel wall in front of us. At first I don't see anything but gray bricks and green slicks of algae. Relief washes over me. I close my eyes and squeeze Sam's hand.

"Shit," Woody mutters, and my eyes shoot open again. I search the wall until I see what he's talking about.

A *door*. My lips part in a nervous smile. The tunnel walls jut up against hard gray steel. I hadn't noticed before because it's the exact color of the grimy bricks surrounding it, and the edge of the wall is flush with the door. But it's there. I grab Sam's arm. I suddenly feel like my legs might collapse beneath me. We're saved.

"Thank God," Shana says. Below us, still crouched in the murky water, Aya moans.

"Sweetie, it's just a door," I say, reaching for her arm. She jerks away, cupping her hands over her ears. She mutters something under her breath that I can't quite hear. "Do you see it?"

"She'll feel better when we get her out of here," Sam says. He gives my hand one last squeeze, then drops it. "Promise."

There's a rickety metal scaffold beneath the door. Dozens of rusted pipes twist along the wall beside it. Sam grabs one of the pipes and hoists himself out of the water. He eases himself onto the scaffold.

"Feels sturdy enough," he says, crawling to his feet. The metal creaks beneath him but holds.

"It must be an old construction door," Woody explains, wading across the tunnel.

I hurry over with him, ignoring the water splashing against my legs. It's past my knees now, and it makes my cold, wet jeans cling to my thighs. I shiver and cross my arms over my chest, thinking of my deep bathtub at home. As soon as I get back, I'm filling it with steaming hot water and bubbles. *If* I get home, I remind myself. I say a silent prayer. *Please let this work.*

Sam sets the candle down on the scaffold, and Woody scrambles up next to him. He twists the doorknob and pulls.

"Jammed," he mutters. He groans, and pulls harder. *"Shit."*

The hope inside my chest flickers. "Jammed?" I repeat.

"Don't worry. We'll force it if we have to." Woody anchors himself against the wall and tugs. But the door doesn't budge.

"I'll help," Sam says.

"We all can, right?" Shana adds. She pushes through the water and climbs up onto the scaffold. "Maybe it opens in?"

"You want to try kicking it?" Woody asks. Sam shrugs and throws his shoulder against the door. The steel frame creaks.

"I think it moved," Woody says. They all start kicking and pushing against the door. I glance behind me, at Aya. She's still huddled at the other side of the tunnel, muttering under her breath and rocking.

"We're gonna die, we're gonna die," she whispers, staring at the door.

"I'm going to help them," I tell her, but she doesn't look at me. A desperate sob escapes her lips. She wraps her arms tighter around her chest.

"We're gonna die . . ."

I turn around, scrambling onto the scaffold with the others. It's the size of a small patio, maybe four feet square. I squeeze next to Woody. Shana and Sam crowd on the other side.

"On three," Woody says. He holds up one finger, then two, and on three we all throw our bodies against the door.

I slam my shoulder into the steel door, and pain shoots up my arm. My shoe slips over the damp metal and my ankle twists beneath me. I tip backward to regain my balance, but I lean too far and tumble into the water.

"Casey!" Sam shouts.

Oily black water crashes over my face and seeps into my ears and mouth. I sink to the bottom of the tunnel and smack my head on the train tracks. Pain flickers at the base of my skull. I open my mouth, gasping for breath, and water floods my lungs. It tastes like vomit. Stomach churning, I push myself to my knees and fumble for the ledge.

I break through the surface and gasp for breath, heart pounding. I'm more disgusted than scared. The water coats my skin.

I dry my eyes with my hands and pull myself to my feet just as Woody launches himself at the steel door. It swings open, and he stumbles through.

"Yes!" Shana cheers. Woody regains his balance, and Shana throws her arms around his neck. "Thank *God*!" she screams.

Sam turns to me and says something, but I'm not paying attention to him. I'm staring through the door. Two tiny dots of light blink in the darkness, like Christmas lights.

"Guys," I say. Two more lights appear. And then eight. Dozens. Hundreds. Horror rises in my throat.

They're *eyes*.

I stumble backward and my foot slips on the subway floor. Just before I crash into the water again, I see hundreds of rats pour from the doorway.

EIGHTEEN

RATS SPILL FROM THE DOORWAY, THEIR BEADY
eyes glowing in the light of Woody's phone. Coarse gray
fur covers their dirty bodies. Their noses twitch in the air,
catching our scent.

I try to stand, but fear makes my legs jerky and stiff.
There are too many of them. They crawl over each other
in a swarm of writhing bodies and pink tails. The sound
of gnashing teeth and high-pitched squeaking echoes
around us. I expect them to be afraid, to run in the opposite direction. Then a large rat breaks away from the pack
and darts at me. I realize something right before it digs its
sharp, yellowed teeth into my skin:

They're hungry.

Stinging pain shoots through my arm. I scream and
yank it away, slipping on the algae lining the tunnel floor.

My feet slide out from beneath me. A sea of rats rushes to the edge of the scaffold, saliva dripping from their teeth. They're the last thing I see before I crash below the water again. Distantly, I hear my friends screaming. Then water rushes into my ears, blocking them out.

Rats pour over the sides of the scaffold, dropping into the water, and their furry bodies sink toward me. Horror rolls through my gut. I open my mouth to scream, but water floods my lungs and I start to choke instead. Darkness flickers at the corners of my eyes. I grope around in the water for something to grab on to and my fingers graze matted, wet fur. Teeth dig into the flesh between my thumb and forefinger. Pain shoots up my hand.

I grit my teeth to keep from screaming, and shake the rat from my hand. Clumsily, I break the surface of the water. Scaly pink tails whip against my cheeks. They feel like razor blades lashing at my skin. I cover my face with my hands, and the rats crawl over my arms and shoulders and get tangled in my hair. Their claws prick my skin. They squeak and scream into my ear.

A rat slips through my fingers. Its teeth dig into my cheek.

A splash echoes behind me. Tremors rumble through the floor.

The rats fall silent. I feel their bodies trembling as they leap off me and plop into the water. I throw myself away from them and scramble to my feet, shaking so badly my knees knock together. I swat at my arms and shoulders. I still feel their feet on my skin, their tails in my hair.

Another splash. Ripples spread over the water. Cold fear oozes through my bones. I whip around, peering into the darkness. The surface of the water goes still.

"Who's there?" I whisper. Shadows gather at the far end of the tunnel. I wobble forward, heart hammering inside my chest. I squint.

Blue tulle bobs along next to the wall. I can just make out the ruffled edges in the darkness. I exhale, and relief pours over me like cool water. It's Aya. I take a step toward her.

"Sweetie?" I choke out when I can finally breathe again. "Are you—"

A hand clamps down on my shoulder. I jerk and spin around.

Sam kneels on the scaffold, reaching down for me. "Come on," he says, offering me his arm. I glance back at Aya, but she makes no move to peel herself away from the wall, and I don't want to wade through the water and coax her out of the shadows. I grab hold of Sam's hand and let him haul me out of the water.

"What happened?" I ask. Woody lies on his back near the door. His phone sits in his lap. The dim light illuminates needle-thin scratches on his face and blood dripping from his chin.

Shana crouches behind the steel door, using it as a shield. A long, deep gash runs down her arm.

"Something scared the rats," she says, her voice trembling. "What could've scared the rats?"

"I don't know," Sam says.

"There was something in the water." My voice doesn't sound like my own. It's thin and distant. "I heard a splash."

I check my back pocket for my phone. My phone's gone, but the pill bottle is still there. I picture the round oxy tablets. *I should toss it into the water, too.* But I don't.

"Shit," I mutter. I peer into the pool, but the water is black as oil. My phone's lost, and Sam's candle lies on its side next to his foot, the flame extinguished.

Woody takes the phone out of his lap. "And then there was one," he says.

I point to the other side of the tunnel, and Woody aims his light at the wall. Water laps against the bricks. I can't make out Aya in the darkness, but the edge of her skirt jerks out of the circle of light and disappears into the shadows.

"Aya!" Woody calls. "Come over here with us."

She doesn't answer. Shana glances over at me. "Someone should go get her," she says.

Below us, a single rat squeaks, then dips below the surface. I cringe, and huddle back against the wall.

"Be my guest," I mutter. Shana creeps out from behind the door, crouching at the side of the scaffold. She looks feral, with her pink hair tangled around her face and bite marks cutting across her cheeks. I stare at her for a beat too long. She's always been wild.

"She'll be okay for a few minutes," Sam says. He drops his hand to my head and pulls his fingers through my damp, tangled hair.

I tilt my head back, studying his face in the dim light. He looks like he got the worst of the rat attack. Bite marks cover his face and arms, and a hole gapes at the collar of his shirt. Pity twists inside my chest. Even after what he did, I still want to smooth the hair back from his face. I want to get out of here and be with Sam and forget this nightmare.

Then I picture him pulling his fingers through Shana's hair, and the feeling fades. I lean away.

A hurt look passes over his face. "Are you okay?" he asks.

"Fine," I say, standing. "Just a few scratches."

"Good." Sam clears his throat. "Let's get the hell out of here," he says.

"Amen," Woody says, pushing himself to his feet.

I scramble to my feet and follow Sam over to the steel door, which still hangs open.

"Thank God," Shana says. Woody's the first one through the open door, and the rest of us crowd around him. He steps inside—then freezes.

"*Shit*," he says.

My breath catches in my throat. "What?" I ask, and

Woody shoves the door all the way open, letting the rest of us see what he sees.

The doorway's been sealed shut. A shallow space opens up just past the steel door, the floor covered in rat droppings and crumpled up newspaper. Past that, a brick wall blocks us in. A small corner of the wall has crumbled away, revealing a tiny hole just large enough for a rat to squeeze through. Now, only weak light drifts through the hole.

The light mocks us. I have no way of knowing whether it's sunlight or some old bulb still burning on the other side of the door. I push past Woody and run my hands over the greasy, dirt-encrusted bricks. I tell myself I'm checking to see if the bricks are rotted, if there's any chance we can tunnel our way through. Tears form at the corners of my eyes, and it's all I can do to blink them back. I curl my hands into fists and pound them against the wall.

"Let us out!" I scream. I pound until my knuckles are bruised and sore. "Let us out!"

"No!" The voice is Shana's. I expect her to pull me away from the wall, to tell me to calm down, but she does neither of those things. She squeezes in next to me, and kicks the bricks with her heavy boots.

"You've got to be kidding me!" she shouts. She kicks again and again, and then she starts pounding with her fists, like me. "Shit," she screams. "*Shit!*"

I collapse against the wall, tears streaming down my

face. I think of the drugs in my pocket and I have to curl my hands into fists to keep from reaching for them. Shana slides to the ground and buries her head in her hands.

Another splash echoes through the tunnel. The hair on my arms stands straight up. "Aya?" I call.

"That wasn't Aya," Woody says in a hushed voice. I turn around, slowly, afraid of what I might see. Woody creeps to the side of the scaffold and shines his cell phone into the darkness. Shana lifts her head and catches my eye. Her skin has gone perfectly white. I feel like my stomach has lodged itself in my throat.

We all wait, staring into the black. The silence around us is absolute.

"Guys," I whisper. "Where'd Aya go?"

The others turn in place, searching the water. She was *just* here. Woody shines his phone out over the water, but the surface stays still.

"Do you think she ran back down the tunnel?" Shana asks. "Maybe she tried to double back to where it wasn't so flooded."

"Maybe," Sam says. I lower myself back into the water, cringing as the greasy cold slips over my legs.

"She was right over there two minutes ago," I say, pointing to the opposite wall.

"Here," Woody says, handing his cell phone to me. "I'll check farther down the tunnel, but I'm fine looking in the dark."

"Thanks," I say, taking the phone from his hands. Shana and Woody climb down from the scaffold and follow the tunnel in opposite directions. Shana hesitates for a second, her eyes on me.

"Careful," she says. It sounds, oddly, like a threat. Sam climbs into the water behind me as Shana drifts away.

"Aya!" I shout. Sam splashes over to the other wall.

"Aya!" he calls, his voice growing faint. I glance over my shoulder, watching him disappear into the darkness. Goose bumps climb my arms. I'm alone. I try to call out, but my voice catches in my throat and I barely make a sound.

I swallow. "Aya!" I say again, louder this time. The shadows feel heavy around me. Like they're hiding something. I jerk my light over the water, but I can't illuminate the whole tunnel at once. Darkness oozes closer. I pull my turtle pendant out from under my shirt and rub the shell between two fingers.

"Aya?" I whisper. I know she's here. She didn't run down the tunnel like Shana thinks she did. I can *feel* her.

I wade forward, the cool water lapping against my legs. There's a flicker of movement at the corner of my eye. A ripple appears in the water.

I spin around. The ripple cuts across the tunnel, only a few inches from my leg. I picture someone hiding beneath the surface of the pool and cover my mouth with my hand, trying to hold back the scream rising in my throat. I shrink back.

A water snake lifts its head from the water. It's no thicker than my pinkie and less than a foot long.

"*Nerodia sipedon,*" I whisper under my breath. I remember the name from the bio class I took at the community center last summer, when I still thought I was going to go to college and study marine biology. It's harmless. I exhale and collapse against the tunnel wall, wishing I was in that classroom right now. Or at Madison's, or, hell, even in rehab. The snake swims past, its tongue darting from its mouth. I cringe and turn back to face the far wall where I last saw Aya.

I sweep the beam of Woody's phone across the tunnel. Flat black water stretches before me. My friends' voices boom off the tunnel walls. I shuffle forward, listening. There's another sound below their shouting. It's a very faint, low rustle, like someone crumpling a paper bag.

Or someone breathing.

I move slowly through the water, toward a thick patch of shadows. I imagine Aya huddled in a corner, whispering silently as she rocks back and forth. I raise the cell phone.

"Nothing this way!" Woody calls. I flinch and spin around, and my light hits him instead. He cringes and shields his eyes.

"Sorry." I move the light, and it sweeps past something floating in the water. Frowning, I wade forward and aim my light.

A gray crescent-shaped object bobs in the water below me. It's roughly the size of my hand, the inner edge serrated like a knife. One end is jagged, like it's been broken.

I frown. It reminds me of the thing I saw on Lawrence's back. But that was a hallucination. I remember the way it dug deeper into Lawrence's skin before disappearing. Impossible. I kneel to examine the object more closely.

Cold fear seeps through my skin. This thing isn't a blade. It's a claw.

A really big claw.

I swallow, trying to imagine how large an animal would have to be to have a claw like that. Nausea fills my stomach.

"Guys," I say, my voice trembling. "I found something."

Water laps against the claw, sending it spiraling away from me. I straighten, and aim the dim light of my phone after it.

The low, raspy sound of breathing reaches me again, raising the hair on the back of my neck. I turn and stare into the darkness. The sound cuts off abruptly. Like someone holding their breath.

I clench and unclench my hand, ignoring the sweat gathering on my palm. The darkness seems to pulse, but I'm too terrified to lift the phone. I keep the light trained on the green sludgy water below.

"Aya?" I whisper. No answer.

Water ripples around my legs. There's someone there.

I can just make out the shape of a body in the shadows. Horror roots me to the spot. I rub my thumb over the side of Woody's phone, steeling myself. The darkness moves, and my breath catches in my throat. I have to see who it is. I have to know.

I lift the phone.

Aya floats into the beam of light. Her legs have sunken below the water, so only her torso and head are visible. Blood streams from her nose and the corners of her eyes. Her cheeks have swollen to twice their normal size. She opens her mouth, and a wet gurgle bubbles from her lips. "Aya!" I slosh through the water and crouch beside her. Her bloodied, unfocused eyes dart around the tunnel. They fix on me, and the sweat on the back of my neck goes cold.

Her normally black pupils burn an icy blue. Terror pulses inside my chest. Something stares out at me from behind Aya's eyes. But it isn't Aya. The only word I can think of is *evil*.

I stagger backward, but I'm not fast enough. Aya rakes her long, manicured fingernails across my cheek, drawing blood. Bright, hot pain rips through my face. I scream, and Aya follows my voice. A blue tint creeps over her skin.

"No!" I grab Aya's shoulders and shake. She doesn't move. Whatever thing crept inside her has gone, and now her eyes are vacant. I pull her from the water, surprised by how easy it is to move her. She feels light—too light.

190

Horrified, I look down at her torso.

Her legs haven't sunk below the water. I was wrong. I jerk away from her and stumble backward, feeling like I might be sick.

Her body ends just below her ribs and her stomach and legs and everything else is *gone*. Broken bits of bone jut out from the bloody stump of her torso. Intestines float on the surface of the water, surrounded by a darkening pool of blood.

NINETEEN

MY SCREAM ECHOES AROUND ME, MAGNIFIED BY
the stone walls and still water. My friends call out but I
can't make out what they're saying. Static fills my head,
blocking my brain with a steady stream of white noise.
This can't be happening. It's another hallucination.

But Aya stares up at me, her eyes clouded and bloodshot and *real*. Her blue-tinted skin is close enough to
touch.

The phone in my hand flickers off, leaving me in the
dark with Aya's ruined body. Fear races over my skin.

"Casey?" Woody shouts. My friends splash toward me. I
think, dimly, that I should move. Run, maybe. Or at least
turn Woody's phone on so I can see if Aya's body has
floated away.

But I can't move. A tangle of emotions hits me all at

once. I want to grab Aya by the shoulders and shake her until she wakes up. But then I think of the wild, hateful thing I saw behind her eyes, and I feel the stinging cut she left on my cheek. It makes me want to put as much distance between myself and her body as possible.

I stumble backward, grabbing for the wall to keep myself from slipping. I feel claustrophobic, like the tunnels are shrinking around me. There's nowhere to run. We're trapped down here, trapped with this thing that's killing us off one by one. I see the ragged stump of Aya's body, burned on the insides of my eyelids.

Bright red blood. Skin shredded like paper. Intestines floating on the murky water. She'd been ripped in half. Something *tore her body in half.*

No person could've done that.

I squeeze my eyes shut, but she's waiting behind my closed lids. I see those icy blue pupils and flinch, remembering how she scratched me. Aya wouldn't have done that. It was like something else was controlling her. Like she was possessed.

Sam grabs my shoulders and spins me around. He finds my hand and tugs the phone from my fingers. A bright light shines in my face. I cringe backward, blinking.

"Casey?" Sam shakes me. I hear the terror in his voice. "Casey, what was it? What did you see?"

I try to speak, but I can't think of what to say. I think of the neon blue eyeliner winging away from Aya's brown

193

eyes, and a sob bubbles up from my throat. Something ripped her body apart, and we can't outrun it or hide from it. Aya's final words echo through my head: *We're gonna die.*

"We're gonna die," I whisper, out loud. I watch Sam's eyes widen, mirroring the horror I feel.

"We're gonna die!" I scream. My whole body trembles. Legs. Arms. Everything. Sam's fingers tighten around my shoulders, but I can't stop screaming. I need to warn them. I need to make them understand. "We're gonna die! We're gonna *die!*"

"There's something over there," Shana says. Sam tosses Woody the phone, and he aims the light over algae-covered bricks and black water. Sam puts a hand on my shoulder and pulls me to his chest. I bite back a scream and breathe deep. He cups the back of my head with one hand, smoothing down my hair. My hysteria cools to a low, flickering panic. I sink into him, watching Woody and Shana over his shoulder.

I know they've found Aya's body when Woody's back goes rigid. He levels his light at something bobbing in the water and releases a strangled, desperate gasp.

"Holy shit," he hisses. He jerks the light away, but not before illuminating Aya's mutilated corpse. A fresh sob tears through me. Sam tightens his grip on my shoulders to keep me from collapsing.

"Oh, God." Sam pulls me to his chest, hugging me so

tightly that it feels like my ribs might splinter. "Oh, God," he says again, his voice shaking. He buries his face in my shoulder. I feel his ragged breath against my neck.

Shana tries to move around Woody. He twists, blocking Aya's body from her view.

"Don't," he warns, his voice barely a whisper. "You don't want to see her."

The muscles in Shana's back tighten. "Get out of my way, Woody," she says, her voice cold. Woody swallows, then moves aside.

Shana freezes. She's facing away from me, so I don't see her expression, but it's like the life drains from her body. Her knees buckle and her shoulders drop. She falls to her knees, grimy water sloshing around her hips.

"Shana!" Woody grabs her by the arms and drags her back to her feet.

"Damn it!" Shana screams. She beats at his chest with her fists, but Woody doesn't let go. "Damn it, Aya. What did you do?"

"It wasn't her fault," I say, but my voice is quiet. Shana's face crumples, and she sinks into Woody's arms.

"What could have done this?" she whispers, but Woody just shakes his head.

"I don't know," he says. The crescent-shaped claw flashes into my head, its serrated edge crusted with blood.

I jerk away from Sam. "We have to go."

Sam's hand freezes on the back of my head. "What?"

"We have to run." My voice sounds ragged. I imagine that giant claw ripping into my stomach, shredding my skin. "We have to go. *Now.*" I splash across the tunnel. My heart thuds in my chest. I think of the ripples spreading over the surface of the water, the rats suddenly racing into the darkness.

A human being couldn't have done that to Aya's body. It was vicious.

Monstrous.

Horror grips my chest. "Something's here," I yell. "*Run.*"

I grab Shana's hand and drag her down the tunnel with me. She stumbles, and I yank on her arm, pulling her up again. Sam and Woody tear after us. Their panting breath echoes off the walls, and water splashes around our legs.

The water rises higher, sloshing up past my knees, and then my thighs. I force my legs forward. Blood pounds at my temples.

The light from Woody's cell phone bounces over the walls, illuminating graffiti and mold. But this isn't normal graffiti. There are no words scrawled across the bricks, no messages or gang signs.

There are just symbols. Strange, alien symbols. I stare up at them, and my horror sharpens. Pain slices through my leg. One of my shoes slips from my feet. I hesitate.

Shana tightens her fingers around my hand. "Hurry!"

she hisses. I kick off the other shoe and lurch forward, my knee throbbing. Water sprays my chest and neck and seeps through my shirt.

The tunnel veers to the left. Woody charges ahead of us—then skids to a stop. He spins around, swearing. Water sloshes at his hips.

"What was that?" he hisses.

"Don't stop!" Shana drops my hand and pushes the hair back from her forehead. I collapse against the wall next to her, struggling to catch my breath. Sam doubles over, panting.

"We have to keep going," I say.

Woody clutches his cell phone in front of him. The light makes eerie shadows across his pale skin and wide eyes. His wet T-shirt clings to his chest.

"I heard something." He raises a trembling finger and points down the tunnel. "Over there."

We all turn. A perfect sea of oily black stretches behind us. Woody aims the light down the tunnel. Our shadows loom long over the dark water. The sound of our ragged breathing bounces off the walls.

"There's nothing there," Shana says.

The light in Woody's hand flickers off. Darkness rushes in around us. Shana inhales sharply, and Sam swears under his breath.

"Shit!" Woody shouts. "My phone! Something grabbed my phone! Did you fucking see that?"

"What are you talking about?" Shana backs into me, groping for my hand.

"Something grabbed my fucking phone," he insists. "It reached into my hand and took it."

"There's no one here," Sam says. But he doesn't sound so sure.

Something flickers under the water. I frown, taking a step closer. Seconds creep past, and I feel my friends growing nervous around me. Shana clears her throat. Woody swears.

"Quiet," I murmur. I hold my breath, waiting.

"Casey . . ." Sam starts. "Maybe we should . . ."

Woody's phone screen flashes back on, just for a second, when it hits the bottom of the tunnel. It illuminates something round and thick. I squint. The surface is mottled and gray. It looks like an old tire.

The tire twitches, then unfurls. Veins ripple along its rubbery flesh. Curled spikes line the gray scales, each as long as a kitchen knife.

I stumble backward, my heart beating in my ears. It's a *tentacle*.

The tentacle moves beneath the water like an eel, and I realize I can't see where it's coming from or where it ends.

The phone blinks off again, leaving us in darkness.

TWENTY

"RUN," I GASP. I GROPE IN THE DARKNESS, GRAB-
bing the first thing I touch. It's Sam's arm. He stiffens
below my fingers. "Run! Run! Run!" I scream.

My friends don't have to be told twice—we all saw that
thing unfurl below the water. There's no time to get our
bearings or argue about which direction to go. We run
deeper into the tunnels, trying to get as far from the tentacle as possible.

Woody stumbles into my back, and I hear Shana panting. Sam twists his arm around so he can grab my hand.
He's faster than me. He pulls ahead, but he doesn't let go
of my fingers.

There's movement below the water, and something
slithers past my leg. I release a desperate shriek and run
faster. Cold splashes around my knees, slowing me down.

My legs used to be lean and muscular, but it's been too long since I played soccer. I grit my teeth and force my legs through the water.

Pain shoots up my bad knee. I breathe through it, trying to ignore the nausea that fills my stomach every time I put pressure on my leg. I will my body to move faster. *Faster.* I'm stronger than this, I tell myself. I used to run *miles* without stopping. Now I'm out of breath after minutes, and my heart feels like it's trying to hammer through my chest.

This isn't just my injury. This is the drugs. I feel how they've changed my body, made me slow and weak, and I hate myself. I feel the oxy in my pocket and the shame makes me run faster. Every time my knee burns with pain, it's a reminder that I deserve this. I did this to myself.

I hear my friends breathing in the darkness around me. Water sloshes against the tunnel walls, and the sound echoes behind us. We're slowing down. I want to shout at them to move faster—we can't stop now—but my own breathing's too heavy. I can't even speak.

Something brushes against my ankle underwater.

I scream, my voice shrill and horrified. Something rustles in the darkness.

"Casey!" Sam hisses. He fumbles for my hand, his palm slick with sweat.

"Run." I push Sam and he stumbles a few feet, water splashing around his waist. I can't stop picturing that

tentacle twisting below us. I imagine it winding around our ankles, pulling us under the surface. "We *have* to keep moving!"

Sam hesitates. "We need a plan, Case. We don't even know where we're running."

"He's right. We're going to get lost if we keep going like this," Woody says, panting. His long blond hair lies flat against his head, and his shoulders are rigid. "I think we left it back there, anyway."

"There could be more than one," Shana says. She's trembling so badly that her voice quivers. "And we don't know how big it is. That tentacle . . ."

Shana swallows, not bothering to finish her sentence. "It could be anywhere," she says, instead.

"What the hell *was* it?" Woody swears, and kicks the water, sending a spray across the tunnel. It hits my cheek, making me flinch. "Where did it come from?"

No one answers. No one knows what it is.

"There's something else," I say. I touch my fingers to the scratch Aya left on my cheek, remembering the thing I saw behind her eyes before she died. Lawrence's eyes had looked like that when I stumbled into him in the tunnel. And then, seconds later, I found Julie's body.

"I think it can do things," I say. I blink, and my eyes start to adjust to the darkness. I can just make out the lines of the subway walls, and the shadowy shapes of Shana and Woody. "I think—"

Something moves in the darkness above them. My breathing sounds raspy in the tunnel. Hollow. It could be my imagination, I tell myself. The shadows playing tricks on me. But the shape looks fluid and muscular, like an elephant's trunk, or a snake dropping from a tree.

"It's *here*," I hiss. I grab Sam's arm and tug right before something crashes into the water where he was standing.

Shana screams. We all tumble into one another, half swimming, half running through the tunnel. The water sloshes up past my waist now. The walls curve to the side and we follow their path around and down another passageway. I don't know how fast that thing can move, but I tell myself that it's slow, that we're leaving it behind.

Still, Shana's words echo through my head. *There could be more than one. And we don't know how big it is . . .*

The air down this tunnel feels stagnant, somehow. Stuffier than before. I grope through the space before me, and my fingers brush against cold, moldy bricks.

"No," I say, sliding my hands over the wall. My heart-beat quickens, and I take a deep breath, trying not to panic. Sam, Shana, and Woody crowd around me, searching the wall for an opening.

There isn't one. We've reached a dead end.

"That thing led us here," Shana says. Her voice quivers. "It was a *trap*."

I take a step back, wrapping my arms around my chest.

The shadows keep transforming into giant, curling ten-tacles. Everything that brushes against my arm or leg is the monster reaching out to grab me.

I rub my eyes with my palms, trying to shake the nerves away. It isn't here yet. It *can't* be here. I blink into the darkness. My eyes blur as I try to make sense of the shadows. I notice a darker patch of black just a few feet above our heads.

I touch Sam's shoulder. "There," I say, pointing to the wall. "Do you see it?"

He moves his hand, fumbling along the wall above us. "There's something here!" he shouts. "It feels like a win-dow or a ledge."

Shana releases a sharp breath.

"Thank God," she says.

Woody splashes over to the wall next to Sam. "I feel it, too," he says. Water sloshes around his waist as he rises up on his tiptoes. "There's a concrete ledge just above our heads. It's narrow, though. Maybe a foot deep."

"What's on the other side?" I ask. Woody shakes his head. The movement is barely a flicker in the darkness.

"We'll have to climb up to see," he says.

"I'll go first," Sam says. He crouches down and releases a grunt as he leaps out of the water. His hand slaps against damp concrete. Woody takes his leg and pushes, helping him scramble onto the ledge. I see the shadow of his body straighten above us.

"There's something over here," Sam says. "It looks like another subway station."

"Is there a way out?" I ask.

"Can't tell," Sam says. "Woody, you help the girls climb up, and I'll pull them over."

Woody blows air through his teeth. "Got it." He turns to Shana. "Come on. You're up."

Shana shuffles forward, and Woody helps her up to the wall. Sam grabs her arms and pulls her onto the ledge, groaning. She scrambles up next to him, then peers over the other side.

"Here goes nothing," she mutters, and jumps. I hear a splash.

"It's deeper over here!" Shana shouts, her voice muffled by the wall. "Hurry!"

"Your turn," Woody says to me. I wade over to him and he grabs me around the waist.

"Who's going to help you over?" I ask before he can lift me.

"You're underestimating my incredible manliness," he says. Then he releases a very manly grunt and lifts me out of the water. I brace my bare feet against the wall to steady myself, and Sam's hands clamp around my wrists. He pulls me onto the ledge next to him.

"You okay?" he asks. I nod and pull myself up.

"I'm good." I leap to the other side, bracing myself for the impact. Water splashes over me. I sink like a rock and push myself off the floor, bobbing back to the surface. Shana's right—it's much deeper on this side. With my head above the water, I have to stretch my legs out all the way to reach the floor. And even then, only my toes skim the thick metal train tracks.

I wipe the water from my eyes and try to examine the space. It's too dark to see much, but the ceiling arches above us, and chipped paint covers the walls. I can just make out a few faded signs on the walls, but it's too dark to read what they say. Once upon a time, this must've been an actual subway station. A platform rises out of the water like an island in the middle of the ocean. I see a staircase twisting up into the darkness. Hope rises inside me.

"It's abandoned, I think," Shana says. Her head pokes out of the water next to me, her pink hair plastered to her skull. "A ghost station."

"You think there's a way out?" I ask. She shrugs, her shoulders rising and falling below the surface of the water. All I hear is her ragged, tired breathing.

"Casey," she says. "I'm—"

Someone splashes into the water next to us, interrupting her. A hand grazes my leg, and I scream, leaping to the side. Woody's head pops through the surface.

"Sam's coming," he says, spitting a stream of water through his teeth.

I step up to the wall and press my hand against the

bricks. I turn my face toward the opening, waiting for Sam. I feel the slightest brush against my pinkie. I freeze.

Fear makes my body numb. I squint into the darkness, trying to separate the shapes from the shadows. But everything is black.

"It can't be here," I whisper to myself. We climbed a wall. We're in a separate station now. It isn't possible. But I move my hand over the wall, just to be sure.

I feel bricks and mold and dirt. The wall is slimy beneath my fingertips, but the slime doesn't bother me anymore. My breathing returns to normal.

Then my fingers brush against something cool and slick. Every nerve in my body flares.

"No," I whisper, groping at the wall. It feels like a fire hose. I pray that it's not what I think it is, that I'm being paranoid. But then it flinches, and something sharp scrapes against my palm. A claw.

I recoil in horror. Sam jumps from the ledge, and a shallow wave crashes into me. He surfaces, his breathing ragged.

He glances at the opening and shudders. "I saw something."

"There's a tentacle," I say, pointing to the wall. Something heavy and wet slaps against the bricks, cutting me off. I can't even feel the cold water sloshing around my chest.

"The tunnels are infested." Shana gasps. "We have to get out of the water."

I force myself to move, and we all swim toward the platform. Sam reaches it first and lifts himself out of the water in one easy motion. I lag behind. A dull ache throbs beneath my kneecap, dragging me down.

A sound like a suction cup unsticking echoes from the wall behind me. Claws click against the bricks. My terror hardens into adrenaline. I grit my teeth, pushing through the pain.

Sam turns, grabbing the nearest arm he can reach— Shana's. He pulls her out of the water, and suddenly she's gasping on the platform next to him.

A splash bounces off the walls. I whip around, peering into the darkness. My breath comes in ragged, terrified gasps.

"Come on," Sam shouts, motioning for me and Woody. We're still a few feet away from the platform.

"Hurry," Woody says. He's ahead of me, but he stops to let me catch up. I try to push myself, but my knee throbs, and the water pushes against me.

I lurch toward the platform, gasping. I see something flicker out of the corner of my eye, and I whirl around. The water behind me ripples. Then goes still.

"Casey," Woody yells. "Come on."

"Right." I turn back around and reach for Sam, but my hand slips out of his. I fall backward, crashing into Woody. Water splashes against the far wall.

"Shit," I mutter. I'm shaking so badly I can hardly stand. Woody pushes me upright again.

"Concentrate," he says, his voice steady. "Don't be scared."

I breathe deep and reach for Sam again. This time I get a good, solid grip on his hand. He pulls, but I'm not as tiny as Shana is, and he's not strong enough to deadlift me out of the water. I try to find a foothold on the platform, but my bare feet slip off the side.

I hear another splash in the water—closer this time. I swear under my breath and squeeze Sam's hand. His fingers are wet and his eyes widen as I start to slip away.

"Don't let go," he says, tightening his grip. I hear something in the water, and my hands start to tremble.

"Come on, Case," Woody says from behind me. He grabs my leg and pushes me onto the platform.

For a long moment I lie there, gasping for breath. I still feel the greasy water all around me, clinging to my skin like a living thing. Sam grabs for Woody, but he's not strong enough to pull him out of the water on his own, and Woody doesn't have Sam's upper-body strength. He can't pull himself out, either.

"Shit," Woody groans. The muscles in his arms tighten as he pulls. I push myself to my knees and crawl back to the edge. I'm reaching for Woody's arm when I see it.

The water behind him swells, then forms a crease. I stiffen. Something's there.

I push myself to my feet and grab Woody's arm.

"Hurry," I say. Woody's arm is wet and hard to keep

hold of. The ripple in the water moves closer. I see some-thing white flicker just below the surface. Next to me, Sam flinches.

"Casey," he murmurs.

"I see it," I hiss back. The blood drains from Woody's face.

"What?" he asks, his voice shaking. "What do you see?"

"It's nothing." I readjust my grip and repeat what Woody said to me just seconds ago. "Concentrate . . ."

Woody opens his mouth. "I—"

A tentacle whips out of the water and pierces Woody's back. I hear a heavy, wet sound. Like raw meat hitting a wall. Woody groans, and his mouth forms a perfect circle.

"No!" I scream. Blood oozes over Woody's teeth. In the darkness, it looks black. He tries to exhale, and specks of blood fly at my face and cheeks. It feels warm and tacky on my skin.

I cringe but hold tight to Woody's arm. His hand goes slack in mine. A crunching sound echoes around us. Woody's body starts to quiver. Blood darkens the front of his T-shirt and spreads across his torso.

A sob escapes my lips. I watch in horror as sharp gray claws burst through Woody's chest. They carve through muscle and flesh, and crush his bones as easily as if they were toothpicks.

Blood pours from Woody's open mouth, falling over his chin and neck. The tentacle whips out through the hole in his chest. Claws flare away from it and dig into Woody's skin like a grappling hook.

Woody gasps, trying to speak. The tentacle wrenches his body below the water before he can utter his last words.

TWENTY-ONE

"NO!" I DROP TO MY KNEES AND CRAWL TO THE edge of the platform. The surface ripples. I search the black water for Woody's blond hair and bright Hawaiian shirt but see nothing. He's gone.

A dark, hopeless feeling seeps through my skin and into my bones. Julie's gone. Aya's gone. And now Woody. My breathing comes fast. Ragged. We still haven't found a way out. We're trapped down here with this . . . *thing.*

I thrust my hand into my pocket and pull out the Tylenol bottle. The pills rattle around inside. The sounds makes my heart beat faster. There's no reason to be good anymore. No reason to try. This is the end.

I wedge my thumb below the lid and pop the bottle cap off. The plastic disk drops into the water, floating on the surface for a second before it sinks into the black. I tip the bottle into my hand.

Strong arms wrap around me and pull me away from the edge.

"What the hell are you doing?" Sam yells. I think he's talking about the pills, but then he pushes me to the center of the platform, casting an anxious glance back at the water. "You want to get yourself killed?"

Yes, I think. I close my eyes and imagine how easy it would be to give up. No more running. No more trying to escape. No more watching my friends get ripped apart. I shake the pill bottle, and a single oxycodone rolls onto my palm.

It's so small. Just a tiny white pill. But it means so much.

A sob bubbles up in my throat. Giving up won't solve anything. I close my fingers around the pill, then fling it into the water. I throw the bottle in after it.

"I should have helped him." Even as I say the words, I picture the tentacle ripping through Woody's chest, the blood spurting from his mouth.

"You think I'd still be standing here if there was any way to help him?" Sam says. His eyebrows furrow and a muscle in his jaw tightens. "He was my best . . ."

Sam's voice hitches. I've never heard Sam cry before. The sound makes my chest hurt. He kicks the column Shana's leaning against, and concrete crumbles to the ground.

"Oh, God," Shana murmurs, lowering her face to her

hands. Her shoulders shake with silent sobs. Sam swears, his face crumpling. Guilt washes over me.

"I should have let him climb up first," I say. Sam's head snaps up.

"Don't say that." He wipes his cheek with the back of his hand, his eyes red and swollen. "Woody wouldn't have wanted that."

Woody would have wanted to live, I think. Nervous energy buzzes up my arms. I start to pace in small, tight circles. Two steps in one direction. Two steps in the other. There's nothing we can do. Nowhere we're safe. I pull my hands through my hair, my fingertips brushing the peach fuzz on the side of my head.

We're going to die down here.

"We can't just stand here," I say. "That thing . . . that thing will . . ." I press my hand over my mouth.

"Casey." Sam pulls me to his chest and wraps his arms around my shoulders. But I don't want to be comforted. I try to step away, and he holds me tighter. I slam my fist against his chest, but he still doesn't let go.

"Don't," I say. My chest rises and falls, rapidly, and I dissolve into tears. The sobs tear through my body, making me weak. I collapse against Sam, giving in.

It feels so good to cry. All the fear and anger I'd been clinging to rushes out of my body, leaving me hollow and empty. I don't have the energy to be afraid anymore. I don't have the energy for anything.

Sam moves his hand in circles over my back. "We're going to get out of here," he promises. "No one else is going to die."

I sniffle. "How can you know that?"

"Because I won't let it happen."

His voice sounds so certain. I almost believe him. I breathe in and out, and in again, and blink my eyes dry. *No more crying*, I tell myself.

"I think I'm okay now." I pull away from Sam and wipe the last tears from my cheeks. Wet curls fall over his forehead. A fringe of dark lashes rim his light brown eyes.

His voice floats through my memory. *You're acting like you don't remember what happened.* I thought he was talking about the day he broke up with me, but he wasn't. He was talking about the black spot in my memory.

"Sam," I whisper. I steel myself, trying to be brave. If we're going to die down here, I have to know about that night. "Tell me what happened the night before I went to rehab."

Sam frowns, studying me. "You don't remember any of it?"

"I remember getting ready to go out," I tell him, seeing the moment clearly in my mind. I'm standing in front of the full-length mirror in my bedroom, fixing my hair. I take a pill for my leg—just one. I don't want to get high, just ease the pain in my knee.

Then the image flickers. Everything goes black. I press

against the darkness in my memory, trying to figure out what happens next. But there's nothing.

"After that, all I remember is waking up in the hospital," I tell him. A flush creeps over my face, and I look down at my bare feet, embarrassed. "I thought I had a bad reaction to the pill. But my parents thought I OD'd."

My breath catches in my throat. I've never had the nerve to ask the next question, but I force myself to say the words now. I can't die not knowing. "Why did they think that?"

Out of the corner of my eye, I see Shana lean forward, listening.

"Your mom called me that night at, like, four in the morning," Sam explains. "She was all freaked out because you didn't come home."

"So you came to find me?" I ask.

Sam shrugs. "Yeah, well, I knew where you guys liked to go. But I checked all the usual spots and you weren't there. Then Julie told me to stop by Sid's. She said you and Shana had been buying from him a lot."

I cringe, picturing Sam in his mom's station wagon. It doesn't really surprise me that we ended up at Sid's that night. I let Shana talk me into the harder stuff after Sam dumped me. And Sid sold it to us cheap.

"I thought Julie was crazy," Sam continues. "As bad as things got, I never thought you'd be stupid enough to hang around someone like Sid. But I went by his van, and you were passed out in back. There was . . . vomit all dried on your cheeks. You weren't moving. I thought you were dead, but then Shana tried to give you a shot of tequila and you started choking. God, I've never been so relieved."

"*Stop.*" The word cracks in my mouth. I hug myself, shivering. I was wrong. I don't want to know what happened. I think of Rachel's cloudy eyes and Tori Anne's rotting teeth. I think of all the girls I heard screaming in the night.

I thought I wasn't like them. But I'm *exactly* like them. An addict. A junkie. Sam catches my eye, and his jaw tightens.

"That was the worst night of my life," he says.

"I'm sorry," I whisper. Chills race down my arms. I hate that Sam was the one who found me. All this time I've been wondering how I ended up down here. How Shana did this to me.

But *I* put myself here. All this is my fault.

"God, I'm so sorry," I say again. Sam grabs my shoulders.

"I didn't let you die then," Sam says, looking into my eyes. "I won't let it happen now."

He turns, abruptly, and walks to the edge of the platform. He leans over the side, searching. I stare at his back.

"Casey?"

I turn at the sound of Shana's voice. She's huddled near

a pillar in the middle of the platform, as far from the edge as she can get. Her blond-and-pink hair hangs over her face in wet clumps, and she has her knees pulled up to her chest, her arms wrapped protectively around them. Her shoulders tremble, but I don't know whether she's crying or shaking. I walk over to her.

"You okay?" I ask.

She shrugs. "I guess." A tear slips over her cheek, but she brushes it away—angry. She glances at the water. "What do you think it is?"

I stare hard at the surface of the water, looking for any movement, any ripple. But it stays still, hiding the horrors below. "I don't know," I say. "A monster, I guess."

"Where did it come from?"

Terror thrums through me, but it's faint, like an echo. "Maybe it blew in with the hurricane," I say, but I don't know whether I really believe that. All that matters is that it's here. It exists.

Shana shudders and glances at me sideways. "Must suck. Being stuck down here with the two people you hate most."

"I don't hate you, Shana," I say, sitting down next to her.

"Why not? I'd hate me." She nods at Sam. "Especially after hearing that."

"Shana . . ."

"No, really." She draws in a breath. "I was *there*, Casey.

I saw how messed up you were and I didn't do shit. I gave you a shot of tequila."

I stare down at my toes. "I know," I whisper.

"You *should* hate me. You should want to know why I did those things. You should scream at me!"

I clench my eyes shut, trying to cool the anger bubbling below my skin. "*I* took the pills, Shana. I knew exactly who you were and I hung out with you anyway. Because I thought you were exciting. Because I was bored with my old life, I guess." I sigh, and curl my toes into the concrete. "You didn't ruin me. I ruined myself."

Shana stares at her waterlogged boots. "If it wasn't for me you never would have ended up in rehab. Ever since we've been down here, I've thought about things a lot. Things I've done. I've been . . . I've been really messed up, Casey. I wanted you to be really messed up, too."

I stare at Shana. I think about asking her whether she was the one who slipped the oxycodone into my Tylenol bottle, and a flare of anger rises inside me—then dies almost immediately. It doesn't matter whether she did it or not. If I wasn't an addict, the oxy wouldn't have tempted me.

"You were trying to sabotage me."

"No. It's not like that." Shana squeezes her eyes together. "Or maybe I was. I don't know. I just wanted you to be bad, too. Perfect Casey Myrtle. If you were drinking and using, then maybe it wasn't so bad. Maybe *I* wasn't so bad." She's quiet for a long moment. I think she's done talking, but then she glances up at me again.

"About what happened with Sam . . ." she says.

"Don't," I say. I'm not ready to talk about Sam.

"I didn't want to hurt you," Shana continues. Her voice cracks. "I just wanted to know what it felt like to have someone like *that* want me."

"Lots of guys want you, Shana," I say.

Shana laughs, but there's no warmth in the sound. "Yeah. Lots of guys want to hook up with me. Or they want me to get them some X, or tell them who my dealer is. But Sam's not like that. When he was with you, he just wanted *you*. I always wished someone would look at me like that."

I stare at my hands, a million feelings rushing through my head. Shana completely changed my life. But she's like a wild animal. There's no controlling her, no telling what she'll do next. I got myself into this mess. But wild animals are still dangerous.

"I'm so fucked up," Shana says. She squeezes her eyes shut, and tears leak down her cheeks. Her shoulders start to shake. "I ruin everything I touch."

"Shana, no." The anger inside me melts. I pull her into a hug, and she sobs on my shoulder. "You just need to make some changes. We both do."

Shana pulls away. Her eyes are rimmed in red. "You think I could ever get clean?" she asks.

"Maybe." As soon as the word is out of my mouth, I realize I don't believe it. Shana might try to get clean, but she never will. She craves the insanity. She thinks it's an adventure.

Her lower lip trembles and her eyes look small without all her usual makeup. She seems so fragile right now. It's hard to believe how dangerous she really is. Sam was right—if I were really serious about getting better, I wouldn't hang out with her anymore. But she's my friend.

I wipe a tear away from her cheek with my thumb. "I could help you," I say. "If you want."

Footsteps pounds against the platform behind us, and I flinch, suddenly alert.

Sam races over to us. His face is flushed red—excited.

"I think I found a way out," he says.

TWENTY-TWO

"THIS WAY," SAM SAYS.

I push myself to my feet, wincing at the dull pain in my knee. Shana moves her hand to my elbow. It's a small, automatic gesture—just enough to lessen the pressure on my knee as I find my balance.

"Thanks," I say. Shana shrugs.

"Don't mention it," she says. But she leaves her hand on my arm as I stretch and bend my leg, making sure my knee is strong enough to walk on. Sam watches, and a frown line appears between his eyebrows.

"Are you all right?" he asks.

"It's just the old war injury acting up." I take a few steps away from Shana, and my knee doesn't even wobble. I breathe a sigh of relief. "It's fine. You said there was a way out?"

The frown lines disappear from Sam's face. He takes my hand. "Come on," he says, and he leads us to the edge of the platform, right next to the moldy tile wall. Water laps at the concrete and spills over. I take two quick steps back. Gravel pinches the bottoms of my bare toes, and I try not to wince. Shana hovers behind me, afraid to approach the water at all.

"You have to come closer." Sam motions to the wall on the other side of the train tracks. "Look."

Shana shuffles forward, and we both move to the edge of the platform. The flooded train tracks stretch away from the station and disappear down another dark tunnel. I squint into the shadows. I see gray bricks, black water.

And a ladder.

I gasp, and throw a hand over my mouth. The ladder stretches from the black pool to the tunnel ceiling, where a metal manhole cover winks down at us. Light oozes in around the edges. *Daylight.*

"Shit," Shana says. "Not exactly easy to get to, is it?"

She's right. The ladder juts off a wall deep in the tunnel. Our platform ends only a few feet from where we're standing, and a narrow ledge stretches down the wall into the tunnel beyond it. The ledge is maybe a foot wide, and chunks of concrete crumble off it and into the water. To get to the ladder, we'd have to creep along that ledge for about a hundred feet. And then we'd have to swim to the other wall.

"I can't." I look from the ledge to the still black water below. Ripples wrinkle the surface. Sam takes my hand.

"It's the only way out," he says.

"We don't know that. What if the cover's stuck again?"

Sam squeezes my fingers, and horror rises in my chest. *Right.* If the cover's stuck, that's it. Game over.

We all die.

Shana takes my hand, weaving her fingers through mine.

"Remember taking the wheelchairs down Henderson Hill?" she asks. I bite my lip, remembering Shana's blue-tipped hair and creaky wheelchair. The way she glanced back at me and winked before launching herself down the cliff.

"You were so brave," I say.

"Bullshit." Shana squeezes my hand. "I was a freaking *wreck.* I thought I was going to die."

"No." I frown, remembering. Shana gives me a sad smile.

"I was just trying to impress you. Maybe shock you a little bit. I didn't know you'd come down after me," she says. "You were fearless."

"I wasn't."

"You *were,*" Shana insists. "You got this look in your eye before you rolled down that hill. I remember thinking you could do anything."

I dig my teeth into my lower lip, staring down into the

water. I think of how my heart dropped when I tipped my wheelchair over the side of that hill, and the dizzy, soaring feeling I got when I started to pick up speed. I felt invincible. Like I could fly.

"You can be brave now," Shana says.

I nod, and step onto the narrow ledge. My legs shake so badly I can hardly move them, but I inch my feet forward, staring down at the water for signs of life. I imagine tentacles bursting up from the depths, wrapping around my body. I can almost feel the cold slap of water as I'm dragged below the surface.

But the pool stays still. I hold my breath, edging farther into the dark.

Sam steps onto the ledge next, and then Shana. The concrete shifts under my toes. I grab Sam's arm, digging my nails into his skin. He holds me, tight.

"Okay?" he asks.

I nod, and take another step.

The platform crumbles beneath my feet. My hand slips from Sam's arm, and my bad knee buckles. Pain slices up my leg and all my nerve endings flare. I howl and drop to a crouch. My knee slams into the concrete. I hear a dull, sickening crack and picture bones splitting, tendons snapping.

Nausea washes over me, and black spots blossom in front of my eyes. I grope for something to steady myself, but my fingers slip off the damp concrete. I tip backward, and my stomach drops as I start to fall.

"Casey!" Sam lunges for me, but he's not quick enough. I spill over the side of the platform and hit the surface of the murky water.

It rushes over me, dragging my body to the bottom of the tunnel. I smack against the train tracks, and my eyes fly open. I peer through the pool, but all I see is black. There's movement next to me. I flinch and grope in the darkness.

I move my feet over the tunnel floor and try to kick back to the surface. My leg roars with agony. I grit my teeth and kick my good leg, but the other drags me down.

I blink, and the darkness separates into murky shadows. The tunnel wall comes into focus. It's close enough to touch. I dig my fingers into the crevices between the grimy bricks, and hope rises in my chest. I can climb out of here. I run a hand along the wall and pull myself to my knees. I reach above my head to grab for the wall again, but my hand lands on something else.

Something muscular, with scales like a snake.

I recoil, and panic rises in my chest. The tentacle slithers over the wall, nothing more than a blurry shape in the darkness. I spot another one a few feet away, twitching closer, and another spread across the ground just inches from my knee.

The water shifts. Something glides past me. I jerk away as another tentacle unfurls next to my face, its curved claws grazing the skin on my cheek.

I can't breathe. My vision blurs. Shana was right—the tunnels are infested. The monster is everywhere. Its tentacles cover the walls and the ground like weeds. I claw at the water, pressing my lips together to keep from inhaling.

Something slides against my back.

I scream and water floods my lungs. Something large glides toward me, cutting through the water with ease. It's too dark to make out more than hazy shapes and shadows, but I think I see thick, glistening teeth and something long and slimy. A tongue.

I squeeze my eyes shut and, for some reason, I think of Rachel, my old roommate at Mountainside. I remember her bloodshot, vacant eyes and the dried vomit clinging to her chin. I used to think that was the worst way to die.

Now I know better.

I open my eyes again and kick, making one last attempt to swim to the surface. But the pool churns around me, holding me down.

Something grabs me from behind, pinning my arms to my sides.

I try to scream, but the water swallows my voice.

TWENTY-THREE

THE CREATURE MOVES CLOSER. MUSCLE CON-
stricts around me, squeezing the air from my chest. Bright
lights blossom in front of my eyes, warning me that I'm
about to lose consciousness. I struggle, but the *thing* only
squeezes me tighter. The water around me shifts as the
creature stretches its jaws. I brace myself to feel teeth ripping into my skin . . .

Suddenly I'm yanked to the side of the tunnel and
dragged, gasping, to the surface of the water. Sam's face is
the first thing I see. Beads of water cling to his hair and lips,
and his skin looks pale. I realize he jumped in after me.

Something slithers past us. The water ripples. I curl my
fingers around Sam's sopping wet shirt.

"We have to get out." I gasp, my throat still raw from
choking. Pain roars through my leg and I'm suddenly

overwhelmed with nausea and exhaustion. My eyelids flicker.

"Casey!" Sam yells. He holds me against his chest with one arm and pulls us toward the wall with the other. He collapses against the ledge, gasping for breath.

"Help her," he moans. Shana plunges her arms into the water and wraps her fingers around my slippery wrists. I dig my toes into the side of the wall and start to climb.

Something curls around my ankle. I grit my teeth and kick the side of the wall, ignoring the pain that shoots up my shin. It recoils and releases me, and I scramble back onto the ledge.

My injured leg flops beside me, useless. I'm afraid to move it, worried it will send another wave of pain through my body. Sam clings to the side of the ledge, still half submerged in the water. His eyelids flicker closed, and his jaw clenches.

"Sam!" I grab Sam's arms, and his eyes shoot back open. I pull, trying to drag him up onto the platform with me, but he's too heavy. "Get out of the water! Hurry!"

"I'm coming," he says, but he moves too slowly. I glance from his face to the water behind him. The surface is still, but I think I see something dark twisting below.

"Hurry," I murmur, my eyes following the shadows. Sam lifts his body out of the water, groaning as he shifts all his weight to his arms. His T-shirt clings to the muscles in his biceps. He pulls one knee up and props it against the ledge, his other leg still dangling in the pool.

Something flickers in the corner of my eye. I flinch and look around, but there's nothing there. My chest tightens.

"Sam," I hiss, grabbing for his shoulder. Shana takes his other arm and starts to pull.

"I'm okay, I'm okay," he mutters, easing the rest of his body onto the ledge. He pulls his other leg out of the water. I breathe a sigh of relief and collapse back against the wall. *Thank God.*

"I saw it," I say in a strange, strained voice. Now the surface is still, but I remember the feel of tentacles sliding over my back. "The monster. It's down there."

Waiting for us, I think.

"I know," Sam says. His jaw tightens. "I saw it, too."

Shana swears beneath her breath. "But you got out," she says. "You're both okay."

Sam meets my eye. "We were lucky," he says.

I press my lips together and nod. I'm more worried about my leg. I tear the ripped fabric of my jeans and press my fingers into the skin around my knee, finding the edges of my kneecap. It's swollen and tender, and a purple bruise blossoms over my skin. I slip a hand under my calf and gently reposition it so my leg stretches out beside me instead of dangling into the water. I inhale, then carefully push myself up onto my good knee, trying to pull the other leg beneath my body.

A sharp knife of pain slices through my knee and up my thigh. Tears spring to my eyes.

"*Shit.*" I lean back against the wall. I try to focus on breathing, but the pain overwhelms me. I dig my fingers into the concrete and try not to scream.

"Casey?" Sam crouches beside me. "Casey, look at me."

I ease my eyes back open and find Sam's face. Pain throbs below my knee like a second heart. Sam studies my leg beneath my clinging, drenched jeans. He lightly touches his thumb along the muscles and bones.

"Does this hurt?" He finds the edges between my knee-cap and shin and presses down. White-hot, blinding pain tears through my leg. It feels like someone wedged a fork under my kneecap and popped it off. I scream and yank away from Sam. I almost fall into the water again, but Shana grabs my arm, steadying me.

"What the hell did you do that for?" Shana hisses at Sam.

"I had to see if she could put weight on it," Sam says.

"It's pretty obvious that she can't put weight on it!" Shana's voice sounds annoyed, but her eyes are wide with fear. She shakes her head and mutters, "Jesus."

"I don't think I can stand," I explain once the pain has subsided a little. "I can barely move."

I look down the tunnel. The ladder is still about fifty feet down and all the way on the other wall. The tunnel's only a yard or two across and not even that deep, but it might as well be the size of a football field. I won't make it two feet with my leg like this.

The water swells and a line ripples down the length of the tunnel. Fear climbs my throat. I scoot away from the side of the ledge and press my back against the wall. The ripple vanishes.

"You can't stay down here," Sam says.

I watch the water for movement, but the surface stays still. The thought of staying down here for even one more second is enough to make me want to curl up into a ball and cry. But it's the only way.

"You two need to go and get help," I say. "You can come back for me."

"I'll carry you," Sam says.

"I'll just slow you down!"

"We aren't leaving you here with that *thing*," Sam shouts.

I open my mouth and then close it. I'm too tired to argue with them. For a moment none of us speaks. Water drips from the ceiling.

"It's settled, then," Sam says. He pushes himself to his feet and groans, leaning against the wall for support. His breathing sounds ragged.

"You're hurt," I say. Sam shakes his head.

"Pulled a muscle," he says, straightening. "It's nothing."

"Let me see." I grab the corner of his T-shirt and pull him toward me before he can protest. Something dark and warm stains the back.

"It's blood," I say, my voice trembling. I touch Sam's back and he flinches.

"It's just a scratch," he says, pulling away. "I'll be okay."

"That didn't look like a scratch!" I repeat.

"It's fine. We'll deal with it when we're out of here, okay?" Sam grabs my hands and squeezes. He tries to look reassuring, but I can see the pain tugging at the corners of his eyes and pinching his mouth. He's right, though. We can't do anything about it in here.

"Okay," I say. "Let's get out of here."

Shana stares out over the water. "You two should go first."

Sam crouches next to me and slides his arms around my waist. I clench my hands at the base of his neck. He stands, pulling me up to one foot. He cringes.

"Sam?" I loosen my grip around his neck and stumble backward, automatically setting my injured leg down to steady myself. Another wave of pain washes over me.

Sam grits his teeth through his own pain. His arms tighten around me. "Casey, stay with me, okay?"

I nod. I need to be strong. I can do this. I wrap my arms around Sam's neck, and he lowers both of us into the pool.

I shiver as the water creeps up my legs and weighs down my jeans. The instant the cold hits me, a chill I can't shake spreads through my body. That thing is down here with us. I imagine tentacles coiling around our bodies and long, curved claws darting at our skin.

Sam pushes off from the wall. I wind my arms around his shoulders, clinging to his back. We glide over the surface of the pool, and I remember him telling me that his dad had a house up by the lake, and that he used to swim there every summer.

I think of that story as I watch his arms slice through the water, propelling us forward. We make it across the tunnel in just three quick strokes. He reaches for the ladder, and I hear clanking metal as he wraps his fingers around the rungs. I tighten my arms around his neck. Sam pulls us out of the pool. Water drips from my clothes and my hair, and I shiver where the cool tunnel air hits me. We did it. We're across.

Something splashes behind me, and I flinch before realizing Shana must've leapt into the water, too. I blink and try to find her in the pool. I see Shana's head duck below the water, and she disappears into the blackness.

I pinch the inside of my palms to keep from passing out. I refuse to be dead weight, even if Sam is carrying me.

"Shana," I call as we climb farther up the ladder. But she's still below the water, and she doesn't answer. I tighten my grip around Sam's neck. He grunts, and I feel a twinge of guilt, realizing how hard this must be for him. The blood on his back feels warm against my chest.

"Does it hurt?" I ask. Sam's quiet for a moment. His hands slap against metal as he pulls us up another rung.

"Nothing I can't handle," he says.

He climbs higher and higher. The manhole cover is directly above us. If I let go of Sam's neck and stretched my arm above me, I could graze it with the tips of my fingers.

Shana still hasn't broken the surface of the water below us.

"Sam, wait," I say. "Shana's still down there."

"I'm not slowing down, Case." He climbs one more rung. Then another. I stare at the water, my heart pounding. The surface stays still.

"Sam . . ." I say again. We climb up another rung, but this time Sam pauses, his breathing heavy. He grits his teeth together and reaches for the rung above us.

Shana bursts from the water below, gasping. She grabs the rungs and pulls herself out of the water, making the ladder shake.

"Keep going!" she shouts. She climbs quickly—barely tightening her fingers before she pulls herself up to the next rung. Then, halfway up the ladder, her hand slips.

"Shana!" I scream. She gropes at the air, swaying backward. Just when I think she's going to fall, she lunges forward, wrapping an arm around the ladder. I exhale.

"Be careful," I say. She nods, giving me a wobbly grin.

"Don't worry," she says. "I'm coming."

"Just two more," Sam says, groaning. I nod, darkness flickering at the corners of my eyes. My arms loosen around Sam's neck.

"Casey!" Shana shouts. She shakes the ladder, and I jolt awake, tightening my grip again.

Sam pulls us up the last rung and reaches for the manhole cover above his head. I hold my breath, expecting this one to be stuck, too. Metal scrapes against metal, and a circle of blue appears above me. Fresh air rolls into the tunnel.

I close my eyes, relishing the light hitting my cheeks. The air is clear and cool. It smells like grass instead of urine and sweat. The fear I've been carrying all night drains out of my shoulders.

Sam crawls out of the manhole and collapses onto the ground. I roll off him. Grass tickles my cheek and the sun beats against my face. A line of sweat forms below my hair.

"Oh my God," I gasp, pressing my face into the grass. "We're out. We're *finally* out."

Sam rolls onto his back, smiling at me. We seem to be in some sort of park. Water glistens in the distance, and I hear leaves rustle as wind breezes past.

I conjure up my last bit of energy and prop myself onto my elbows, army-crawling back to the manhole. I squint down, but the sudden brightness makes it hard to see anything but black. I blink, and the shadows begin to separate.

Shana's only four rungs down. I exhale, relieved, and start to reach for her when a twitch on the far wall draws my attention. I narrow my eyes.

Daylight pours into the subway opening, slowly bringing the rest of the tunnel into view. Thick gray tentacles cling to the walls like vines. They crawl from the water and curl over moldy bricks, twitching when the breeze gusts past them. I stare, horrified.

Shana's too focused on the ladder to see them. I open my mouth to yell at her to hurry—then hesitate. The tentacles surround her on all sides. They swell and undulate over the bricks, claws curling over scales the color of oil.

They're too close. Any sudden movement, and they'll strike. I force myself to look away, trying to keep my face neutral.

"You're almost here," I say, instead. My voice trembles. I stretch my hand toward Shana and she reaches for me. My fingertips graze her chipped, dirty nails.

"Casey," she says, smiling her too-wide toddler smile. A tentacle unpeels from the wall and curls toward the back of her head.

Shana gropes for my hand. I hold my breath.

A tentacle whips out of the pool, spraying me with water as it twists into the air. Its gray scales look nearly black, and its claws glint in the sunlight.

"Shana!" I scream, but it moves too quickly. My best friend is still smiling when the tentacle wraps around her waist.

Claws flare out from the tentacle and tear the fabric of her shirt. Shana opens her mouth, and a wet gurgle bubbles from her lips. The claws dig into her flesh, shredding the skin on her arms.

She gropes for me, but I'm too far away to reach her. The monster wrenches her off the ladder and drags her down.

"No!" I scream. Shana crashes through the surface of the pool and disappears below the water.

TWENTY-FOUR

MY SKIN STILL TINGLES WHERE HER NAIL GRAZED my finger. Just seconds ago, I was reaching for her hand. And now . . .

The water ripples, then goes still. Something white and ghostly flickers below the surface, and I imagine it's Shana's face. Hope rises in my chest. She's stronger than the others were. She'll fight this thing. I watch the water, waiting for Shana to burst through the surface, gasping.

But the pool stays calm. Bile clogs my throat. I pull my leg beneath me, cringing at the sudden ache, and drag myself onto the ladder. Shana's there. She's still alive, and she needs me.

The metal rungs dig into my palms, and the cold subway air envelops me. I take a deep breath, then tug my leg around and position my foot on the ladder. Bright, furious pain rushes over me. It's so intense that my vision swims in and out of focus. My hands go slack . . .

"Casey!" Before I know what's happening, Sam has his hand around my arm, and he's dragging me away from the ladder. My cheek hits the cold, wet grass.

"Shana!" I sob. I try to crawl back to the manhole, but Sam stops me.

"She's gone," he says. He holds me by the shoulders to keep me from trying to crawl back to the tunnel. I try to pull away, but he holds tighter.

"Let me go!" I sob, pounding my fists against his chest. "I need to save her. I need to save her!"

The last of my energy drains away. I collapse against Sam's chest, tears blurring my eyes. Shana's giddy smile flashes through my head. I hiccup, and fresh sobs jolt through my body. I should have warned her about the tentacles. I should have tried harder to grab her hand.

Sam pushes the wet hair off my face and kisses me on the forehead. "It's okay. We're safe, Casey. You're safe."

"Shana . . ." My voice gets caught in my throat. I huddle closer to Sam, taking comfort in the warmth of his chest beneath his damp T-shirt. Images force their way into my head: Aya's vacant eyes, Julie's bloodstained fingers. I weave my arms around Sam's neck, holding tight. Like I'm afraid he might disappear. His hands find the small of my back.

"It's okay," he murmurs into my ear. "You're alive. You're safe. It's going to be okay."

I'm still trembling when Sam tilts my head back and kisses me. Our lips move together, desperate and hungry. I kiss him so I don't have to think about the look on Woody's face when the tentacle tore through his chest, or Aya's blood-stained dress floating in the water where her legs should have been.

The sun warms my shoulders, and the grass tickles my bare feet. I feel Sam's heartbeat, his breath against my neck.

It's okay, I think to myself. *I'm safe. It's going to be okay*. I press my lips against Sam's, harder, waiting for the memories to grow dim.

Sam's lips freeze on mine.

I jerk away. "What's wrong?"

Sam's eyes widen. His skin turns the color of ash.

"Casey . . . ?" Blood spurts from his mouth and oozes over his teeth and lips.

"Oh my God!" The voice doesn't sound like mine. Sam releases a choked gasp and doubles over, holding himself up with one hand. I grab his shoulder to steady him, and my hands start to shake. He coughs again, spraying the grass with blood, before collapsing onto my lap. A deep red stain pools at the base of his spine. Blood seeps through his T-shirt and spreads up his back. Tears spring to my eyes. I glance down at my own hands, horrified to see blood clinging to my fingertips.

"No." I peel the T-shirt off his back, revealing a deep, ugly gash.

The wound slashes across Sam's spine. It's at least six inches wide, and it gapes open, revealing the raw meat of Sam's back, and bones poking through a thick layer of blood. The skin around the edges has already blackened.

"We need an ambulance," I say. I dimly remember hearing that you have to apply pressure to keep a wound from bleeding out. I press both hands against Sam's back. He cringes, and fresh blood oozes through my fingers.

"Casey." Sam pushes me away. His eyes have a cloudy cast to them. He frowns. "I can't see you."

"Sam?" My voice cracks. "Sam, I'm going to go get help."

"Don't." His fingers enclose my wrist. He's barely touching me, but it feels like every single bone in my body breaks at the same time. I squeeze his fingers.

"Sam . . ." I whisper.

He gives me a lopsided grin. "Did . . . did I tell you Woody's going to let me crash in his apartment . . . after graduation?" He stares at something behind me, something he doesn't seem to see.

"Sam," I whisper. I touch his chin, turning his face so he'll look at me.

"He knows a guy . . . let us play on weekends." Sam's voice gets weaker. I huddle closer, wondering if he still knows I'm here. Tears flood my eyes.

"Don't cry." Sam tries to lift his hand and touch my cheek. He drops it halfway there, pain flashing across his face.

"Don't move," I say. Sam's arm starts to shake, and he collapses back onto my lap. I sob, and brush the hair back from his face. "Sam!"

"You can come, too," he mutters, eyes fluttering.

"No!" I say. "Look at me!"

Sam's eyes lose focus. His limbs go still.

"Sam!" I shake him, but he doesn't move. "Wake up! *Sam*. Don't leave me!"

Agony crashes over me. I gape down at Sam, a silent scream frozen on my face. Static buzzes in my ears, blocking out everything but his final words.

You can come, too.

My arms start to tremble, and I collapse onto my dead boyfriend's chest. A ragged sob claws from my throat. A gust of air brushes over my skin, freezing the water still clinging to my arms and legs.

I burrow deeper into Sam, trying to ignore the chill that's already crept into his body.

"I want to come," I whisper. His T-shirt is still wet, and it smells like sewer. But below that, it smells like Sam. My Sam. I grab handfuls of it in my fists and breathe it in. "Please don't leave me here."

Out of the corner of my eye, I see something move toward me. I stiffen. It's just a jogger. He rounds the corner of the lake, hesitating when he sees me.

"Everything okay?" he calls. I open my mouth, but I can't speak. The black is pulling at the edges of my senses. It won't be long before I fall unconscious. I know I should fight to stay awake, but I can't fight anymore. There's no one left to fight for.

I lower myself to Sam's chest and finally let myself rest.

TWENTY-FIVE

LIGHTS FLASH BEHIND MY CLOSED LIDS. THEN they flash off again.

I feel myself grow lighter and fight against it. It's like swimming. I try to push myself farther, into the deep, fathomless ocean of sleep. My friends are down there. I see their faces in the darkness. Shana is just inches away from me, her bright pink lips parted in a little-kid grin.

"You look deranged," she says. But the current pulls me up. The light grows brighter, and pain seeps in through my arms and legs. It stabs at me like knives. Shana's face disappears.

I open my eyes. It's dark. Blue lights flash from a machine to my left, and an IV stands at my right. Plastic cords connect to my wrists. A velvety night sky stretches beyond the hospital window, and in the distance, I can see the dusky glow of city lights.

Someone's shouting.

I blink, listening. The shouting cuts off, abruptly.

Then: "Female victim. Seventeen years old."

They must be talking about me. Sleep tugs at me. I don't fight it. Everything's so much easier when I'm asleep. My eyelids flutter.

An ER tech pauses in front of my room, his hands resting on a stretcher. Suddenly I'm wide awake. A sheet covers the body, but a bare leg wearing a muddy black boot dangles over the side of the stretcher, along with a single pink-tipped lock of hair.

"Shana," I whisper. I try to push myself out of bed, but my arms wobble beneath my weight, and I crash back against my pillows. Darkness flickers at the corners of my eyes, and before I can move, the morphine pulls me under.

My eyes twitch open hours later, still heavy with sleep. Something woke me. I lie curled on my side, listening for a sound. The machines beep. A car honks on the street outside. A nurse in the hall says something about going for coffee.

My eyelids grow heavier. I'm about to drift off again

when movement flickers at the edge of my vision. My eyes shoot open and I sit up in bed, the mattress creaking beneath my weight.

Someone stands in the hall outside my room, a shadow hovering near the doorway.

"Mom?" My voice cracks. It feels raw and unused. Whoever's watching me doesn't move. I curl my fingers around the scratchy hospital sheets and scoot back against the headboard. My heart thuds against my chest. The shadow shifts.

"Shana?" I say.

Shana drifts forward, dazed. A film of sweat coats her skin, and her hair frames her face in limp, tangled clumps. She wears a hospital gown just like mine. But hers is several sizes too big and the neck droops over her shoulder, revealing deep red gouges on her neck and chest.

"Oh my God." I push back my blankets and climb out of bed. The drugs make me slow and clumsy. The room spins, and I have to lean against the wall for a second to regain my balance. The dizziness subsides and I yank the IV out of my hand, then stumble across the room and grab the door to keep myself steady. Pins and needles race up my injured leg. Gritting my teeth together, I take the last few steps toward Shana and throw my arms around her neck.

"You're alive," I whisper. Tears spring to my eyes. Shana feels small beneath my arms, her bones thin and fragile. I hold her tighter, but she doesn't hug me back. Her hands hang next to her sides, limp.

"Shana?" I loosen my grip slightly, but then Shana jerks her arms around me. Her fingers crawl to the back of my head and press into my scalp. Chipped nails dig into my head.

"What are you doing?" I squirm, but she tightens her grip. Her nails claw at my skin. "Wait, you're hurting me."

I start to pull away, but then I see something jutting out of Shana's back, and I hesitate. The object looks sharp and long as a steak knife, but curved in a subtle arc. I raise a trembling finger as it sinks deeper into Shana's body.

Nerves prickle over my arms and the back of my neck. I push her off me and she stumbles back a few feet, giggling.

"No," I say. She's trying to be funny. This is one of her stupid jokes. The muscle in my leg twitches, telling me to run. I edge backward. "Shana, what the hell is going on?"

The light hits her face, and dread washes over me. Skin droops from her cheeks and jaw. Her mouth stretches. This smile is different from Shana's giddy, little-kid grin. There's no joy in it. It widens, all jagged teeth and bleeding gums. Her normally brown eyes burn icy blue. Just like Aya's had.

"Shana," I whisper. The scratch Aya left across my face flares, like a warning. This *thing* couldn't possibly be the real Shana. Shana's dead. The creature from the subway took her body, just like it took Aya's body, and Lawrence's body.

And now it's come for me.

The creature's blue eyes darken into twin black pools. Something appears from deep within Shana's throat. It pulses and writhes against the roof of her mouth. It pushes on her teeth.

A tentacle uncurls over Shana's cracked lips. It lashes at me, gray scales flashing under the dim hospital lights, and cuts, whiplike, into my cheek. The tentacle crashes into the wall behind me, and the plaster crumbles under its weight.

Terror grips my chest and I run for the door, but Shana darts into my path and pushes me back into the room. I lose my balance and slam into the tile. Pain shoots through my hips.

The tentacle loops around my ankle. Tiny, jagged claws flare out from the scales and cut into my flesh. I scream and kick, but the tentacle constricts and the claws dig into my leg like a grappling hook. I push myself to my hands and knees and start to crawl, but the tentacle yanks my legs out from under me. My forehead smacks into the floor and darkness blossoms in front of my eyes. My head feels thick and dizzy.

I can't move. A shadow falls over me. I can practically picture the tentacle hovering above my head, its claws about to dig into the soft flesh around my neck. I groan and try to roll over, but pain washes over me in waves. A tear forms in the corner of my eye.

This is it. I'm going to die.

Voices sound in the hall just outside my door, but they fade before I can call out for help. Shana's bare feet pad across the floor.

Then, silence.

I roll onto my back. Something flickers at the corner of my eye, and I flinch and throw my arms around my face again, expecting Shana to lunge. But nothing happens.

I lower my arms, trembling. The doorway where Shana had stood is empty. I push myself to my knees, eyes darting around the small hospital room. Did she run away? Or is she still here? Hiding?

The blue machine beeps in the corner. My IV stands next to the bed, cords dangling to the floor. The curtain rustles.

My heart thuds in my ears. I rise to my feet. Pain flutters through my bad knee, making me cringe. The door to the hall is just past the window. If Shana's behind the curtain, I'll never make it.

The curtain moves again. I grit my teeth and creep across the room. The tile chills my bare feet, and my fingers shake. Goose bumps raise the hair on my arms and neck.

I reach forward, grab the curtain, and yank it back—revealing nothing but an open window. A cool breeze drifts into the room, rustling the curtain.

The fear drains from my body. I exhale and peer outside, half expecting to spot Shana racing across the street below. But the glass just reflects my hospital room back at me. I see the blue heart monitor, my abandoned IV, and the rumpled sheets on my bed. I lean closer.

A figure huddles beneath my bed, watching me with hungry eyes.

Terror washes over me. I scream and whirl around as a tentacle whips out from under the bed and slams into my chest. It knocks the air from my lungs, and suddenly I'm sliding across the floor. I crash into the metal hospital cart, and the cart topples. Glass shatters, and medical supplies rain down on me. I throw my hands over my face.

Shana skitters out from under the bed on all fours. She moves like an insect, her arms and legs jerky and disjointed. I try to stand, but Shana crawls on top of me, pinning me down with her legs. She leans closer, her face inches from my own. Her mouth slackens and droops open with the weight of the writhing tentacle.

The tentacle curls around my neck, pinching my skin. I gasp for air and dig my hands into the scaly mass. I try to pull it away, but the tentacle is solid muscle. It tightens around my neck until my head grows light. Shana grabs my wrists and slams them against the ground.

I kick and push against her arms, but Shana's too strong. She doesn't even seem to notice me struggling beneath her. I inhale, and a tiny bit of oxygen trickles into my lungs. Then the tentacle constricts, crushing my throat.

"*Let . . . go . . .*" I gasp. Darkness blurs the edges of my eyesight.

Shana cocks her head, considering me. It's a strange, reptilian gesture. Another tentacle oozes from her mouth and slithers toward my arm, coiling around my wrist. Dizziness overwhelms me. I open and close my mouth.

Shana unhinges her jaw, and another tentacle slips past her lips and hits my chest with a hard, wet thud. It feels like an oily rope. I cringe as it gropes along my skin and tightens around my throat. My head pounds. The room starts to go black.

The room flickers in and out of focus. The realization hits me: Shana is going to kill me. This *monster* is going to kill me. I'm going to die if I don't do something. I move my arms and jerk my head forward, smacking Shana on the forehead. Pain oozes through my skull, but she just blinks, surprised, then shifts her body forward so she can hold my head down with both hands.

She crouches over my good leg, pinning it to the floor. I grit my teeth together and shift my bad leg out from under her. Pain throbs beneath my kneecap. Nausea rises in my throat. I choke it back and drive my ruined knee into Shana's chest.

Shana flies off me. Her tentacles uncurl from my arms and neck, and whip back toward her mouth. Pain like fire burns through my leg. I push myself to my feet. The ache makes my head throb. Out of the corner of my eye, I see Shana moving toward me with that same jerky, disjointed crawl. I hobble for the door. The nurses' station is just down the hall. If I can get out of this room and shout for them, I might be able to save myself. Pain shoots up my leg with every step I take, but I bite my lip and push myself through it. The hospital door yawns open. Just three more steps. Two more.

"Help!" I gasp. "Someone, please!"

A tentacle shoots out of Shana's mouth and wraps around my ankle. An agonized scream rips from my throat. I leap for the door, but the tentacle pulls me down. My cheek slams against the tile and, for a second, all I see is black. I groan, and try to push myself back to my feet. The room swims around me.

Shana crawls toward me. She's twisted her arms around so that her hands face the wrong way and her elbows jut out to the sides. Her bones stick out at bizarre angles, pulling her skin taut. Empty eye sockets stare out from opposite sides of her head, and her mouth widens, taking up her entire face. Sweaty pink hair falls over her forehead and sticks to her cheeks.

I try to move my leg, but everything below my waist has gone numb. I grope along the ground for something to help me pull myself up, and my fingers find the cool metal bars of the hospital bed. I grab hold and pull. My muscles burn, but I'm not strong enough to stand. My legs flop beneath me—dead weight.

Shana closes in on me. I grope along the ground for a weapon, and my fingers find a long rubber cord.

The emergency call button.

I yank on the cord, and the button clatters to the ground. Shana leaps for me, but I grab hold of the button before she lands on my chest. She digs into my shoulders with both hands and shoves me to the floor.

My head smacks against the tile. Drool drips from Shana's lips and plops onto my cheek. I press the emergency button, but it's too late.

Shana lowers her face. *This can't be the end*, I think, and then I wrap the cord around the monster's throat. I pull tight, tighter.

Spit bubbles around Shana's mouth. I stare at her neck so I don't have to look at her face. I pull the cord tighter. Her skin goes pale. My hands start to shake. Shana moves her hands from my shoulders and gropes at the cord.

A strand of pink hair falls to Shana's neck, dislodging something inside me. The color's called Cotton Candy. I helped her pick it out.

It'll make you look innocent, I told her. She cackled, and shoved the dye into her pocket without paying for it.

I could never *look innocent,* she shot back.

A sob builds in my throat. I choke it down and pull the cord tighter, tighter. *This isn't Shana,* I tell myself. *Shana's already dead.*

The monster tries to tug the cord away, but it digs into her and she can't get a good grip. She scratches at her neck, uselessly, leaving deep red scratches on her skin. The muscles in my arms burn with pain. I don't have much strength left. Shana gasps, her fingers still clawing at the cord. I squeeze my eyes shut so I don't have to watch the life fade from her face.

Shana collapses on my chest. The tentacles slither back into her mouth—slowly at first, then fast, like a tape measure snapping back in place. I drop the cord and fall back onto the floor, panting. Tears spill down my cheeks.

The floor beneath me trembles. I stiffen, but it's just footsteps. They thud closer, and then a nurse appears at my doorway.

"Is everything all right in . . . Oh *God!*"

The nurse screams. I try to open my mouth. I want to tell her that it's okay. The monster is dead. It's finally over. But the nurse starts yelling and then another nurse races into the room with a stretcher.

They lift me off the floor and onto the stretcher. They're

talking to me, asking me questions. But it's like someone put the world on mute. Their mouths open and close without making a sound.

Let me go, I think. I try to move my legs, but nothing happens. Panic builds in my chest. I try to lift my foot and then wiggle a toe. My legs stay still.

I can't move.

TWENTY-SIX

THE NURSE'S SCREAMS STILL ECHO THROUGH MY
head a week later as I hobble out of the hospital balanced
on brand-new crutches. I stop next to a concrete pillar
and tip my head back, letting the sun warm my face. The
stiff padding digs into my armpits. I close my eyes and a
memory flashes across my flickering lids.

We need a stretcher, someone yells.

And then, *She's crashing . . .*

My eyes snap back open. I can't stop replaying those
final moments, when I'd been so certain I was going to
die. I stare down at the stiff white cast stretching from my
ankle to mid-thigh. My toes stick out at the bottom. Mom
painted them green last night and drew a tiny picture of a
turtle on the cast near my ankle.

I wiggle my green toes. It's a miracle that I can move them. A miracle that I can even stand.

"Just want to make sure you know what she's taking for the pain, how often, and . . ." Mom's voice drifts out of the hospital, interrupted by the glass doors sliding shut.

". . . I've been a parent just as long as you have," Dad's saying when the doors slide open again. "I'm perfectly capable of giving her medication while you're at work."

They step out of the hospital together and stop arguing when they see me listening.

"I told you guys already." I reposition the crutches beneath my arms and half turn so I can face them. "No drugs."

Mom sighs, and fumbles with her threadbare tote bag. I painted her nails, too, against much protesting that lawyers really shouldn't have green fingernails.

"The doctors said a little ibuprofen is *fine*," she says, "You're recovering from a torn ACL, a major surgery, and . . ."

"No drugs." My voice is stern, and I give her my very best "I'm serious" face. It's something I've insisted on since getting out of surgery. There were a few days when I was too groggy and out of it to keep the doctors from giving me ibuprofen. But now that I'm healthy enough to feed myself and walk with crutches, I've been adamant about refusing all pain relievers—even the ones they say I can't get addicted to. I haven't forgotten the promise I made to myself in the subway. I'm done with all of that.

"If you say so." Mom tucks the pills into her bag, shaking her head.

"How are you feeling, kiddo?" Dad scratches his eyebrow.

"You mean since, like, twenty seconds ago? When you asked me the last time?" I force myself to smile, even though the expression feels unnatural. The therapist I've been seeing for the last few days said smiling would trick my body into feeling happy, but so far, it hasn't worked.

It's not that I'm not grateful to be alive. But the grateful feeling is tangled up with horror and guilt and shock. Like how necklaces get knotted together when you leave them at the bottom of a jewelry box. It's impossible to separate one emotion from the rest.

The smile pulls at the corners of my mouth. "I'm feeling great, Dad," I say. "This is pie."

"Slow down," Mom says, looping an arm around my shoulder. "You need to *rest*."

"Fine," I say. To be honest, I don't care if the crutches are uncomfortable or if Mom acts a little bossy or Dad asks a million questions. I don't care if my knee aches when I'm trying to fall asleep or if physical therapy is grueling or if taking a painkiller would make all this easier. I'd take the pain and the frustration a million times over. It's so much better than the alternative.

Dad opens the car door and starts loading my things into the backseat. I hand him one of my crutches.

"Casey?"

The voice comes from behind me. I turn, the other crutch still propped beneath my arm. "Madison?"

Madison grins at me, holding up a balloon shaped like a soccer ball with the words *Get Better Soon!* written across it in blocky blue print.

"I would have come sooner, but I didn't know if you wanted visitors." She shoves her free hand into the pocket of her bright green jeans and stares down at her scuffed sneakers. The last time I saw her was from the passenger seat of Shana's Buick. Heat climbs my neck at the memory.

"I'm glad you came," I say, offering an awkward smile. "I didn't realize anyone knew I was here." My doctor didn't think I should travel after my surgery, so my parents kept me at the hospital in Manhattan instead of transferring to Philly.

"Are you kidding? Everyone at school is talking about you." Madison shifts her weight from foot to foot, then hands me the balloon. "Anyway, I got this for you. I think it's supposed to be for, like, an eight-year-old boy, but whatever."

"That's so sweet," I say, taking the balloon. It's kind of tricky trying to hold it while also gripping my crutch, but I manage. Madison flashes me a sad smile and clears her throat.

"I also wanted to say that I'm sorry," she says. "For what happened at my party last week and, you know." She takes a deep breath. "Because of what happened to your friends."

I wind the balloon string around my fingers. I still remember the way the ropes groaned as Julie's body swung from the pipes, and how Woody's hand suddenly went limp as the monster burrowed through his chest.

I pull the balloon string tight, watching the tip of my finger turn blue. Aya's last words echo through my head. *We're all gonna die.*

"Casey?" Madison touches my arm.

"Sorry," I mutter, shaking the pins-and-needles feeling out of my fingers. "I try not to think about it."

Madison chews on her lower lip. "I heard Shana took an entire bottle of Ritalin. That's why she killed all those people."

I clear my throat. "She was on a lot of drugs," I say.

"And the cops still think she was responsible for everything?" Madison asks.

"They do." I stare down at my cast. It's not my fault Shana got blamed for the murders. No one believed my story about the monster, especially not after I tested positive for Ecstasy. And the nurses *saw* Shana attack me in the hospital. It all fit together so perfectly.

Except no one could explain the bloody gouges on Shana's arms.

Or why the other bodies were never recovered. Even Sam disappeared in the time that the runner left to get help and the ambulance arrived. His body vanished. Like something had reached out of the subway and dragged him back underground.

I flex my fingers, nearly losing my grip on the balloon. These are the details I focus on. They remind me that I'm not crazy. That what I saw was real.

Madison takes a step closer, lowering her voice. "Is it true that you had to . . . you know . . ."

"Kill her?" A lump forms in my throat. I don't want to think about how I tied the cord around Shana's throat and pulled until she could no longer breathe. My hands tingle at the memory.

It wasn't Shana, I tell myself. *Shana was already dead when they brought the body to the hospital. I didn't murder her. I murdered the monster. The thing that killed her and took over her body.*

Cotton candy–colored hair flutters through my memory. I flinch, letting the balloon string unravel from my finger.

"It was self-defense," I tell her. Luckily, Madison nods. She grabs my hand and squeezes.

"I'm sorry," she says. Awkward silence stretches between us. Madison clears her throat and glances at my knee.

"I heard that you had another surgery," she says. "You're probably benched for good now, huh?"

This time, my smile feels almost natural. It's easier to focus on the medical stuff. The surgeries and rehab have been so challenging that I can go almost five minutes without thinking about Sam's last words or how light Aya felt in my arms. I lean into my crutch and stretch my bulky cast out in front of me.

"Actually, the doctors say I'll be good as new," I say, wiggling my green toes. "I should be back out on the field this fall."

A nervous grin flashes across Madison's face. "You're going out for soccer again in the fall? *Really?*"

"As soon as I'm done with physical therapy," I say.

Madison squeals, and wraps me in a hug. "That's amazing! I can't wait," she says.

"Yeah, well, don't get too comfortable being captain," I say, untangling myself from her arms.

"Bring it *on*," Madison says.

"Casey!" Mom pokes her head out the car window. "We're going to be late for your first physical therapy appointment. Time to tell Madison good-bye!"

Madison squeezes my arm. "I'll see you on the field."

"See you on the field," I say.

Madison jogs back to her car, but she turns to wave at me one last time before climbing inside. I toss my crutch into the station wagon. Dad starts to get out of his seat to help, but I wave him off.

"I got it," I say.

Before I can pull myself into the car, the ground trembles, and I stiffen—immediately alert. A train rumbles through the subway below me.

I stare through a nearby grate, nerves prickling. For a second, I think I see them. Shana reaches out of the darkness, her chipped fingernail grazing my hand. Strobe lights illuminate the tips of Sam's hair and the hard edges of his jaw. Julie tosses back her black curls and fumbles with the onyx ring on her finger.

Then the rumble of the train fades into the distance, and they disappear.

I release a ragged breath, my lips suddenly cold. I see them all the time. Every girl with winged eyeliner is Aya. Every guy in a Hawaiian shirt is Woody. But when I look again, I'll see that the girl is too tall or too thin. The guy is older than he seemed a second ago.

My friends are dead. They aren't coming after me.

That's what I keep telling myself.

ACKNOWLEDGMENTS

THESE ARE ALWAYS IMPOSSIBLE TO WRITE because books are like children, and it takes villages of people to raise them. So thank you thank you thank you to the amazing Les Morgenstein, Josh Bank, and Sara Shandler at Alloy for every single thing you've done to help make this book a thing that happened and not just a fun story I daydreamed about in my apartment. Thank you, Kristin Marang, for all your support on the social media front, and thanks to all the people at Alloy who worked behind the scenes. Also, thanks to Emilia Rhodes. You're my favorite. I'm going to steal you back from Harper if it's the last thing I do.

Huge, overwhelming thanks to my lovely family at Razorbill. Jessica Almon, thank you for the brilliant, insightful notes. Thank you to Casey McIntyre and Ben

Schrank for everything you've done to support me and my words. Huge thanks to Felicia Frazier and Rachel Cone-Gorham and the rest of Razorbill's sales, marketing, and publicity team, all of whom worked so hard to help people discover my books. You guys are wonderful!

And finally, thanks to my fabulous, supportive family and friends. This book is dedicated to Feelings Are Enough, which is my fake band (don't ask; it's exactly as ridiculous as it sounds). Thanks for letting me steal the name, guys. I promise not to release a fake solo album anytime soon.

And, of course, thank you to Ron. Couldn't have done it without you, babe.

FORGIVE ME, FATHER, FOR I HAVE SINNED.

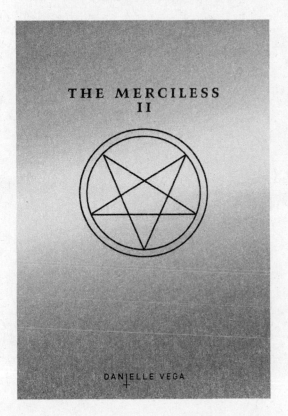

THE MERCILESS
II

DANIELLE VEGA

THE EXORCISM OF SOFIA FLORES

Turn the page for a sneak peek. . . .

CHAPTER ONE

I stand at the living room window, staring at the empty house across the street. A single strand of old Christmas lights dangles from the roof. Half the bulbs have burned out.

A woman and her son lived there until this morning. They didn't even say good-bye, just packed their things and disappeared, like everyone else in this neighborhood. I'm surprised it took them this long. After all, no one wants to live across the street from the murder house.

I exhale, fogging the glass. Rain lashes at the window and turns our yard into a swamp. A red Matchbox car floats down the driveway in a muddy river.

I stare at the churning water and try to breathe, but the air in the house feels thick. It's like inhaling sand. I cup my hands and place them over my mouth, forcing my lungs to draw in a ragged wheeze. I exhale through my fingers and choke down another gasp of air.

Breathe, I tell myself. My eyes flutter closed. *It's just a panic attack.* My chest unclenches, and I take a longer drag through my nose. The room stops spinning. I'm in control again.

I grab my phone off the coffee table. Mom is the first in my short list of favorites. The rest—Grace, Riley, and Alexis—are dead. I cast another glance out the window. Row after row of empty houses stare back at me, the tattered FOR SALE signs perched in their yards like warnings.

I hit Call and a photo of my mom, Sergeant Nina Flores, flashes across the screen. She glares at me over a bowl of cereal, a single Honey Nut Cheerio stuck to her cheek. Normally, her appearance is military-precise, but I caught her before her coffee.

The sight of Mom's face calms me a little.

"Chill, Sofia," I mutter to myself, lifting the phone to my ear.

Mom answers her phone mid-ring. "Sofia?"

"Mom?" Relief seeps through me. "Where are you?"

"I'm still at work, Sof. Is everything okay?"

I clutch the phone with both hands, shooting another look out the window. "I thought you were coming home early today."

"I told Jodi that I'd cover for everyone who took off early for Thanksgiving . . . Why? Did something happen?"

"No, I just—" I glance at the empty house across the street. It was different when I knew there was someone living there, even if she kept her curtains closed and averted her eyes whenever she saw me. "I just don't want to be alone."

Mom is silent for a beat. "Did you have another attack?" she asks, her voice gentle. When I don't answer, she sighs. "Honey, did you try the breathing exercises Dr. Keller taught you?"

I drop onto the couch and take another pull of air. Dr. Keller is the therapist who helped me realize that what happened last summer was a mental breakdown. In other words: *not real*. Because of him, I could finally accept that Brooklyn didn't make blood rain from Riley's ceiling, she didn't set fires with her mind, and she definitely didn't pull out Riley's heart with her bare hands.

He told me that I don't have evil inside of me. Just guilt.

He said that witnessing Riley's murder traumatized me, and I made up a story to cope. And I want to believe

Dr. Keller. But sometimes I can still hear the sound of Riley's heart falling to the ground. I still feel Brooklyn's lips on my cheek.

We don't kill our own was the last thing she said to me before disappearing into the woods. The police never found her.

"The exercises helped, I guess," I mumble into the phone.

Mom exhales. "See? It's like he said after your last session: the most important thing is to learn how to control your fear so it can't control you."

I pick at the skin next to my thumbnail. Brooklyn could be outside my house right now. My guilty conscience may have invented some of what happened over the summer. But Brooklyn was real, and she killed my three best friends.

Dr. Keller can prescribe all the breathing exercises he wants, but even he can't keep me from being afraid.

"How's *Abuela*?" Mom asks.

I shift my eyes to the staircase at the edge of the living room. Grandmother's rosary beads click against her table upstairs like a metronome, slowly counting the seconds. Yesterday, she woke up coughing and gasping in the middle of the night. She had a slight fever and her skin was clammy, but her temperature came down this morning, so we decided not to take her to the emergency room. "She's okay. She's breathing normally and her temp was at ninety-eight point six degrees," I say. "I checked when I got home from school."

"Good. I'm glad she's feeling better." Mom clears her throat. "And how's the rest of your day been?" she asks.

I frown and tug at a thread coming loose from my jeans. "Fine. Boring."

"What, no big Thanksgiving break party?" She's trying to be funny, but her voice sounds strained. She knows I don't have any friends left in this town. Charlie is the only person I still know in Friend, Mississippi, and he hasn't spoken to me since the night I stole his truck and tried to save Riley. I've barely said a word to another classmate since I found Grace's dead body hanging from our shed. The thread unravels, leaving a tiny hole in my jeans. I press down on the fabric, but the hole won't magically knit itself back together. None of the holes in my life will.

"Mom," I whisper, the word cracking in my mouth. "Why do we have to stay here?"

A sigh echoes through the phone. "Sofia . . ."

I blink hard to keep from crying. "Dr. Keller says this environment is toxic for me, and everyone else has already moved away. We could go back to Arizona, or—"

"I'm stationed here, in Friend. I have another sixteen months before I can apply for reassignment."

"But—"

"It's my job, Sofia. You know how the army works. There's nothing I can do."

I lay back on the couch, swallowing the rest of my argument. We've talked about this before. A lot. Silence stretches between us. Wind presses against the glass of the windows, and thunder rumbles in the distance. It reminds me of a car engine, except cars don't drive down this street anymore.

"Sweetie," Mom says, her voice a bit softer, "sometimes I wish we could leave, too. Even I get jealous of how everyone else can pack up and go. Our life is just a little more complicated than that. What's that needlepoint your grandmother has on her wall? Jealousy is cancer, or—"

"*Jealousy is like cancer in your bones,*" I correct her. "It's from the Bible."

Mom releases a small laugh. "Right. Jealousy will eat you up inside if you let it, so let's try to look for a silver lining. Do you think you can do that?"

I shrug, even though I know Mom can't see me. "I guess."

There's a pause. "Look, I might be able to convince Jodi to let me leave a few minutes early," Mom says. "Everyone's already left for the holiday, so there's not much to take care of. How about I swing by China

Garden to pick up some takeout, and we can watch *The Wizard of Oz?*"

A small smile tugs at the corner of my lips. *The Wizard of Oz* is my favorite movie. We watch it whenever I have a bad day. "That sounds okay," I say.

"I'll call ahead and order the usual. See you soon."

"Thanks, Mom. Love you."

"Love you. Now do your homework."

"Roger that," I say, and we both hang up.

Reluctantly, I flip through my dog-eared copy of Shakespeare's *The Tempest* and open up my laptop. My last three schools have all done a unit on *The Tempest.* I could probably recite the entire play from memory. I stifle a yawn and my eye twitches.

The cover of *The Tempest* shows a girl in a blue dress staring out over a stormy sea. She has her back to me, her tangled red hair blowing in the wind. Miranda has been stranded on a deserted island with a crazy magician for twelve years but I'd still trade places with her in a second. Deserted island beats murder house any day.

Just looking at her makes my eyelids feel heavy. I'm supposed to write an essay detailing the major themes and, even though I've read the play *three* times, I can't think of a single thing to write. I stare at the blank Word document on my laptop. The cursor blinks mockingly. The sound of my grandmother's rosary beads echoes down the stairs and, after a second, the blinking and the clicking match up.

Blink. *Click.* Blink. *Click.* Blink.

I tear my eyes away from the screen and pick up *The Tempest.*

The girl on the cover stares right at me, a terrible smile on her face.

I jump up, banging my knee—*hard*—on the coffee table. I wheeze in pain at the shock. The book goes flying and hits the wall with a smack and then drops to the carpet, faceup. My heart is pounding so hard that I want to throw up.

I don't want to look. But I *have* to look. I lift my head.

The cover of *The Tempest* is normal again. Miranda stares out over the sea, her hair teased out behind her. No demon smile. I unclench my fists and stop holding my breath. The nausea has passed.

I sink back onto the couch and pull my computer onto my lap. My knee pulses with pain. I'll have an ugly purple bruise tomorrow, but I won't be able to distinguish it from the others. I've been so jumpy lately that I'm covered in welts and marks.

I lower my fingers to the keyboard and type: *Power and enslavement, the favored and the forsaken, lovers and masters. These major themes of* The Tempest—

My screen freezes. I frown and tap on the keys. Nothing.

"Shit," I mutter. I slide a finger over the trackpad, but the cursor doesn't move. It's not even blinking. I groan and close my eyes, pinching the bridge of my nose with two fingers. This is just perfect. My knee aches, my brain feels mushy, and now my computer's not working. It's like the universe doesn't actually want me to get anything done.

I open my eyes and reach for the power button to restart. A blank window pops onto the screen.

"What the hell?" I whisper. A cursor appears. Someone starts to type.

Hello, Sofia.

Fear curdles in my stomach. This isn't happening. My eyes must be playing tricks on me.

A GIF of a skinned cat opens on the desktop. Flies crawl over its limp, pink tongue, and its cloudy eyes stare out at me from a raw, bloody face. Someone painted a pentagram on the dead grass, and dripping candles form a circle around its rotting body.

Every other sound in the house goes silent. I can't hear the rain or Grandmother's rosary, but my breathing magnifies in my ears until the ragged gasps overwhelm me. I remember the smell of that cat. Milk gone sour. Fish left in the heat. I press the computer's power button, hoping to erase the image that's already seared into my brain. It won't turn off.

Another photograph appears. It's Alexis's dead body, crumpled beneath the second-story window of the abandoned house. I still don't know if she jumped or was pushed. The curve of her twisted limbs is deeply unnatural. A beautiful broken doll. She stares up at the sky, a thin line of blood dribbling from her lips. Her fingers curl toward her palms, as though she's reaching for someone.

I jerk away from the sofa and stumble to my feet, the laptop tumbling to the ground.

"Stop it," I whisper. I back up against the wall as more pictures flash across the computer screen.

A girl holding a butcher knife. Bloody handprints. Cockroaches racing across the floor.

Then a video file pops up, blocking all the other images. A train races toward the screen, headlights flashing. A horn blares, followed by a high, piercing scream. I press myself into the wall behind me, my breath fast and ragged. I'd know that scream anywhere. Karen. The girl I killed.

I squeeze my eyes shut and throw my hands over my ears. "Stop it!" I shout. "Please!"

Laughter echoes through the house.

I open my eyes and spin around, certain I'm going to see Brooklyn standing behind me smiling her terrible demon smile. But I'm alone. The laughing grows louder.

"Please," I whisper. My hands start to shake. I curl them into fists and hug them to my chest. *"Please* stop."

"So-fi-a," someone says in a singsong voice, making the hair on my arms stand up. The voice is coming from the laptop speakers.

"You're one of us, Sofia," Brooklyn says. "I'm coming for you."

"No!" I shout, and I jerk awake, gasping.

I'm lying on the couch, my computer still balanced on my lap. There's nothing on the screen except for a blank Word document and a blinking cursor. The storm beats against the windows and my grandmother's rosary beads click away upstairs. Otherwise, it's dead quiet. My chest rises and falls as I try to catch my breath. It was a nightmare. Just like all the other nightmares I've had since the day Brooklyn killed Riley and revealed my horrible secret. No one else knows that I dragged a girl onto the train tracks at my last school. Not Dr. Keller. Not even my mother.

Tears spill onto my cheeks. I try to wipe them away but they come too quickly, blurring my vision and making my breath hitch. I vowed that I would never think about that night again. It was an accident, a moment of insanity. And, after everything that happened with Brooklyn, I've more than paid for my crime.

I start to do my exercises, but my hands shake so

badly that I can't keep them cupped around my mouth. I grab my phone to call Mom again, then pause.

The time blinks at me from the home screen: 9:47. I click on my recent calls list. I talked to Mom at six fifty-two. Almost three hours ago.

"What the hell?" I murmur. I wipe the last of the tears from my eyes. "Mom?" I call, pushing myself to my feet. "Are you there?"

I listen for Mom's voice, or the sound of her footsteps. There's nothing.

The doorbell rings, making me jump.

Nerves crawl over my skin like spiders. We never get visitors. I take a step toward the door, thinking of vacant eyes and bloody footprints and tattered skin.

I don't want to answer it, but the doorbell rings again.